**Also available from Chantal Fernando
and Carina Press**

The Knights of Fury MC Series

Also available from Chantal Fernando

The Wind Dragons MC Series

The Cursed Ravens MC Series

The Conflict of Interest Series

TEMPER

CHANTAL FERNANDO

carina
press

**carina
press®**

Recycling programs
for this product may
not exist in your area.

ISBN-13: 978-1-335-21593-2

Temper

Copyright © 2020 by Chantal Fernando

This edition published by arrangement with Harlequin Books S.A.

For questions and comments about the quality of this book,
please contact us at CustomerService@Harlequin.com.

Carina Press
22 Adelaide St. West, 40th Floor
Toronto, Ontario M5H 4E3, Canada
www.CarinaPress.com

Printed in U.S.A.

To Tenielle.

For loving my boys just as much as I do.
Most people have a village.
I have you—a fierce one-woman army.
And I'm forever grateful.

Author Note

Please note: This book is part of a series but can be read as a standalone.

TEMPER

Prologue

Five Years Ago

"Can I have a whiskey, please?" the brown-eyed behemoth of a man asks, studying me with a little too much intensity for my liking. He's wearing a black cut over more black clothing, and he smells good, like leather with a hint of cologne. "You have pretty eyes."

"Thank you," I reply, ducking my head. My eyes were always a source of insecurity for me growing up, with them being quite bright and amber in color. To say I was teased about them was an understatement. At school they used to call me a cat and say I was possessed. I don't care what people think about me anymore, a confidence I think comes with age, but that doesn't mean that I don't get embarrassed when someone says something about them.

"What's your name?" he asks, never moving his eyes from me.

"Abbie."

"I'm Temper," he says, then clears his throat. "I mean, Tommy."

"How many people call you Tommy?" I find myself asking, trying to hide my smile. I've heard all of the bikers that pass through use road names for each other. I don't know how many of them actually go by their real names, but it's nice that he offered it to me. I can only imagine why they call him Temper, and if that isn't warning to stay away from this man, I don't know what is.

"Uhh." He tilts his head back, actually considering the answer to my question. "None."

I laugh softly and slide him his drink. "Okay, Temper it is."

Suddenly feeling shy, I start to wipe down the counter while his friend returns from the bathroom and sits down next to him. "You didn't order me a drink?" he asks Temper, unimpressed.

"Sorry, Prez, got a little distracted," Temper replies, sounding amused.

Prez looks at me. "Hey, sweetheart, could I get a beer, please?"

"Sure," I say, grabbing the first bottle I can reach from the fridge. "Is this one okay?"

He nods. "Perfect."

Setting the beer in front of him, he throws some money on the table and smiles. "Thank you."

My mother always warned me about the bikers passing through the bar, and while I have had bad vibes from other bikers in the past, I don't get any from these two. But what do I know? I'm twenty-three and have never even left Nevada. I'm the stereotypical small-town girl, something I always thought I'd never end up being. Our bar is off the major interstate that is one of the only ways to get to Vegas from Southern California and vice versa. Because of our location, we see just about every type of person—truckers, families, young people and bikers.

"What time do you finish work?" Temper asks me as he stands to leave. "Can I take you out for dinner? Or coffee, or something?"

I shake my head, taken aback by his request. "No, I don't think so. But thank you for asking me."

He's older than me; I know that much. If I had to guess, I would say he's in his midthirties, which is maybe why I'm so surprised by the fact that he asked me out. If I'm being honest, while I am attracted to him, the age difference freaks me out a bit. I've been stuck here pretty much my whole life—I wouldn't know what to talk to him about. I'd probably bore him to death. Also, I'm flattered, but I don't think going out with a man by the name of Temper would be a good idea.

"Okay." He nods, brown eyes flashing with disappointment before he masks it. "Have a good night, Abbie."

"You too, Temper," I respond, our gazes holding and lingering for longer than necessary.

Flashing him a smile, I head back into the kitchen to hide, pushing away a slither of regret that hits me out of nowhere. Yeah, he's good looking, but so what? There's plenty of good-looking men out there.

I've never been on a proper date before, and my first one isn't going to be with a man like that.

Chapter One

Present Day

"That man keeps staring at you," Sierra says under her breath, eyes on the cash register. "He's kind of sexy, in an 'I don't know if I'm going to give you the best orgasm of your life or kill you in your sleep' kind of way."

I don't bother looking up, because I already know exactly who she's talking about. Temper, President of the Knights of Fury MC, has been coming into our family-owned bar, Franks, for several years now. He's not a regular—in fact, the MC only passes through maybe once or twice a year—but he's not someone that's easily forgotten.

The last time he was here, he told me that he was now the president because his Prez had died, and he practically cried as he said it. When he asked me out, like he always does each time he is here, I almost caved.

Almost.

"Abbie," Sierra growls. "Pay attention, he's coming over here."

I glance up just as he stands in front of the bar. "Abbie," he says with a nod, smiling. "How have you been?"

"Not too bad," I reply, taking in those brown eyes

and shaved head. I'm not quite being honest. With my mom's declining health, I've had to take over Franks, and had to drop out of college to do so. I spend every day here or at home, helping her as much as I can. My younger sister, Ivy, helps too, but I insisted she stay in college, so she can't always be here.

One of us had to make a sacrifice, and I volunteered. She can still become something, get out of this small highway town and follow her dreams.

"Really? It's been about eight months since I've seen you, and that's all you have to say?" he asks, brow furrowing.

I wish I had something exciting to say, like maybe tell him about a vacation I went on, or a competition I won, anything really, but I have nothing.

"Just work," I explain, smiling sadly. "Mom's not well, so I've had to take over with running the place."

He nods, understanding reaching his eyes. "I see. So you and Ivy work here full time now? What about school?"

"I've had to put that on hold," I admit, and it hurts to do so. I've always wanted to be a lawyer, ever since I can remember, but now it looks like my life is going to be spent serving drinks. When I brought up the idea of selling the place to Mom, you would have thought I had asked her for a million dollars. Franks has been in our family for decades, and it's more than just a bar to her, it's our family legacy. "Hopefully next year or so I can go back."

Temper's lips tighten. "I know how important that is to you."

He's killing me. I can't believe he remembers. Last time he was here, in addition to him opening up to me about Prez, I had told him just how much I was loving my courses. He commented on my excitement over it, telling me it was cute, and he could see just how passionate I was about school. And now here I am, months later, admitting to him how I've basically dropped out to work full time.

"Whiskey?" I ask, changing the subject. The last thing I want to discuss with him is how my life is no longer going according to plan, and I'm here because I need to be. Mom didn't want me to drop out either, but there was no other option, and now I'm stuck.

I always do this. I'm the first to want to help, the first to volunteer myself up, and you know what they say—no good deed goes unpunished. I'm learning how true that is firsthand. It's not like my mom is helping the situation either; she's milking it by just lying around the house feeling sorry for herself. And yesterday she didn't even go to her doctor's appointment. She seems depressed, and it's almost like the roles have reversed and I'm now the parent, and it's a whole lot of stress for me. I wish she would take her health seriously—she did have a stroke—and be responsible. Her doctors have said she will make a full recovery so long as she puts in the work. It's hard running Franks and constantly worrying about her as well.

I'm going to go gray soon, I can feel it.

He nods, and I take the opportunity to distract myself. It's been a while since I've seen him, and he looks good. It's like the man doesn't age. He's tall, strong, and kind of mean looking, but he's been nothing but nice and respectful toward me. We kind of have a routine going every time we see each other. We chat, we flirt, he asks if he can buy me dinner, and I say no. He accepts that and leaves, until next time.

I don't know why I always say no anymore. The first time was a combination of him being a biker and feeling so much older than me. But the age thing doesn't bother me that much anymore. Truth is I've never said yes, to any man, to any date. I get asked out by people coming into the bar, but you don't have to be experienced to know what they are really looking for, and it's not a loving, long-lasting relationship. My experience is severely lacking, aside from prom and the mistake I made after it, and there's no saving me now. I'm going to be a spinster. Hopefully Ivy will give me some nieces and nephews I can claim as my own.

Temper places money on the table, with a huge tip, like he always does. "Seriously? Who tips that much?"

His lip twitches. "You can take yourself out to a nice dinner with it, since I know you're never going to let me take you out."

"You giving up that easily?" I tease, giving him a flirtatious smile. I don't know where this sudden boldness is coming from, other than the fact that I don't want him to stop asking me out, and I've only just realized this.

I've never met another man like Temper, and I don't think I ever will. I see how people treat him, avoid him, and make sure not to challenge him. Hell, my own mother warned me to be friendly with him, but never too friendly. He has this air of menace about him, but over the years I've also seen how he treats his MC brothers like family, and he's always respectful, even to the people who work here. I've seen him vulnerable when he talked about his Prez… Hammer was his name, I think. He's never rude, or arrogant—to me, anyway—and he's always generous and polite. When he speaks to me, he always uses a humble, gentle tone, one that I've come to enjoy listening to. I know there is another side to him, and I can't help but want to get to know that more.

"It only took a few years of rejection," he jokes, lifting the whiskey glass to his lips. I don't think I've ever heard him make a joke before.

"Maybe this was the year I was going to say yes," I reply, clearing my throat. I don't know what's come over me, but I have the feeling like if I truly do want to take a chance and go on this date, it's now or never. I'm stuck here, in the same job, doing the same thing every damn day, and I deserve to have a little fun and do something reckless for once in my life. I've always been the good girl, the trusted daughter, and the responsible older sister, taking care of my family as much as I can, since my dad has never been around. I know his name, Cohen Pierce, and that he lives in California somewhere. But he wanted, and still wants, nothing to do with me, and that's fine. I've accepted that.

But what have I ever done for me? Other than college, which I had to drop out of anyway, I can't think of one single thing.

Temper lowers his glass and studies me, brown eyes filled with surprise and suspicion. "You want to go on a date with me? Why now?"

Shrugging, I lower my eyes to the counter before returning them to him. "Time for me to live a little."

Being safe hasn't gotten me anywhere in life.

Now that I've opened my mouth and said this, Temper looks like he doesn't know what to do. In fact, he looks slightly concerned. "You want to live a little, so you have decided to take me up on the date I've been dreaming about for the last…how many years exactly?"

"Five, I believe," I mutter, and clear my throat once more. "Yes, pretty much, unless you've changed your mind now?"

He smirks. "You're the most beautiful woman I've ever laid my eyes on. I don't think I've ever asked anyone out more than once in my life." He pauses, and then adds, "Actually I can't even remember the last time I asked anyone out, other than you."

That can't be right.

We see each other twice a year at the most, and he's sexy as hell, powerful, and I'm sure he has women throwing themselves at him. And as for me being the most beautiful woman he's ever laid eyes on…

I don't think I'm anything special.

I mean, I know I'm not completely unfortunate in the looks department. I have long dark hair, and a curvy body that most people would consider to be plus sized, and along with my amber eyes and heart-shaped lips, I do okay. Yet I don't think I ever expected to encounter such a compliment.

"I don't know how any of that can be true," I say, shaking my head. "But you can explain it all over dinner. I finish here at seven."

"Seven it is." He nods, flashing me a grin. "I'll be here early in case you decide to change your mind."

"I won't," I declare, moving to serve a new customer that walks in.

I don't know how today took this turn of events, but for the first time in a long time, I'm excited.

Chapter Two

"You're doing what?" Ivy asks as I remove my Franks T-shirt and look at myself in the staff mirror.

"I'm going out for dinner," I tell her again.

"With a man?" she asks, blinking slowly a few times.

"Yes, Ivy, with a man," I say with an eye roll.

She continues to stare at me with wide eyes while I fix my hair and apply some lipstick. "Is it with Ben? He's been wanting to ask you out for months."

"No, it's not," I reply, turning away from the mirror to face her. "Ben?"

"Yep," she says, shrugging. "You didn't get that vibe from him? He asked me what your favorite flowers were and everything."

I definitely didn't get that vibe from him, which goes to show just how oblivious I am with the opposite sex. "It's no one local, just going out for a meal and a chat, no big deal."

"My big sister is finally going on a date and paying attention to men, how is that not a big deal?" she asks, doing a little happy dance, shimmying her hips from side to side. "Now you can stop being such a saint and making me look bad."

I grin. "Not being socially awkward isn't a bad thing. How do I look?"

I'm wearing high-waisted black jeans and a thin sweater—nothing much, but it's all I have to work with without going home to get changed. Luckily, I had some makeup in my bag.

"Stunning," she says, smiling with her eyes. "Is he coming in here to pick you up? Because I'm nosy as hell and am going to be all over that."

Cringing, I rub the back of my neck. I was kind of hoping I was going to get away with leaving with Temper without Ivy seeing, but I know that's not going to happen. "It's Temper," I blurt out. "I'm going out for dinner with Temper."

I don't have to explain who he is, because she knows. Everyone here knows.

Her green eyes widen and her lips part. "You're going out to dinner with the president of the Knights of Fury MC?"

"He wasn't president when I first met him," I mutter, and expel a sigh. "And don't you dare go and tell Mom. You know that she will kill me, and she doesn't need any added stress right now."

"I'm not going to tell Mom, but I'd love to know what the hell is going through your mind right now. You've said no every time he's asked you out. What's changed?" she asks, sounding both impressed and confused. "I mean, I think I'm more of a Saint or Renny girl, but I guess Temper is pretty hot for an older guy."

I hold my arms out. "This is my life, Ivy. All my plans are gone, and I'm going to be working at this bar for the rest of my damn life. There's no becoming a successful lawyer, no traveling and definitely no moving to a different state anytime in my near future. This is the only excitement I'm going to get, so I'm going to take it, and not let another year pass me by thinking about this man yet being too scared to do anything about it."

"You aren't going to be working here forever," she tells me, frowning. "I know it's hard now, and you've had to give up a lot—" She stops and takes a deep breath. "You know what, you're right, you just have a good time tonight. Live in the now and enjoy yourself. Let that big bad sexy biker spoil you a little. Just be safe, and message me to check in."

"I will," I promise, smiling. "And thanks for not telling me I'm an idiot for doing this."

"No judgment here," she replies, arching her brow at me. "But do remember, we don't know where this guy has been so…" She reaches across to the corkboard where there are condoms pinned on it. "You might need some of these."

My mouth opens and closes. "You know that corkboard is a joke, right? The pins are put right through the condom packets. Oh my God, please tell me you haven't actually used one of those before. It's a joke Ben copied after seeing it somewhere."

She blinks at me, confused. I take a deep breath and explain, "The pin is going through the packaging, making a hole in the condom, so whoever uses it will probably get pregnant."

Green eyes widen. "I'm going to kill Ben. And no, I haven't used any of them, but…" She pulls one out of her pocket and throws it into the trash.

I scrub my hands down my face, making sure to avoid my lipstick, and then start laughing. "What the hell am I going to do with you?"

Sierra sticks her head into the staff room. "Your biker is here waiting for you."

"Thanks," I say, puffing out a breath. "And he's not my biker."

They both ignore me. Ivy follows me out and stands next to me as my eyes land on Temper. He looks good, and has even changed out of his T-shirt and into a black collared shirt. It's cute that he's put in a little effort, and when he smiles at me I can't help the butterflies I feel in my stomach.

"Hey," he says, moving toward me.

"Hey," I echo, going around the bar to him. "You're early."

"I told you I would be." He grins, glancing over at my sister. "I'll take good care of her, I promise."

"You better," she threatens in a dry tone. "Have her home by midnight."

"I'm not Cinderella, Ivy," I reply with a small laugh, winking at her and accepting Temper's hand.

He leads me outside to his motorcycle. I've never been on one, but I've always wanted to, and I'm not going to lie and say I haven't thought about being pressed up behind him from the very first time he asked me out.

"You're going to need this," he says, handing me a leather jacket, helping me into it and zipping it up to my chin.

"Whose jacket is this?" I ask him, eying him wearing his own. The one I'm wearing feels and smells brand-new, and looks really expensive.

"Yours," he replies, smiling down at me. "I knew you'd need one for tonight."

"So you went out and bought me one?"

Who does that? And how did he know my exact size? The jacket fits like it was made for me, so he must have a good eye for women's clothing, or he just got lucky.

"Yeah," he replies nonchalantly. "It looks good on you."

Our eyes lock, and hold.

"Thank you," I whisper, looking down and then back at his bike. "So, where are we going for dinner?"

"Well, I checked out all of the options here," he says in a dry tone. My lip twitches. We have two restaurants other than Franks, and none of them are anything special, so we aren't too spoiled for choice. No matter where we go I'm going to likely run into someone I know and get people talking, but so be it. I'm over playing by the rules, and I just want to enjoy myself tonight without worrying about anything else. "And I didn't like any of them, so I got creative."

"Got creative how?" I ask, grinning. I was expecting to go to one of the same places I've been eating at for my entire life, but now he's mixing things up a little, surprising me.

"You'll have to wait and see," he murmurs, handing me a matte black helmet.

I eye it. "Tell me you didn't go out and buy a helmet as well."

"I didn't have a spare," he simply says, then lifts me up by my hips like I weigh nothing, and sits me on the back of the bike. I'm not a light woman, and it takes me a few moments to process this.

Just how strong is he?

I mean, sure, his biceps are huge.

"You ever ridden before?" he asks, bringing my attention from his arms back to his handsome face.

"No," I say.

"Keep your feet on here and off the exhaust," he advises, positioning my boots.

"Do you go to the gym?" I find myself asking him.

"No." He laughs. "I do some boxing with the men sometimes, though. We have our own little gym at the clubhouse, but it's been ages since I've stepped into there."

"Huh," I whisper, slide the helmet on and flick open the visor. I have so many questions I want to ask, like what else the clubhouse has, but now I'm picturing a bunch of hot, shirtless men boxing each other, sweat dripping down their bodies.

Temper is in the center of my daydream.

"You ready?" he asks, hopping on the bike, my breasts pressing against his back.

My arms come around him of their own accord, and they feel comfortable there somehow. "Yep!"

He revs the engine and my fingers tighten, excitement filling me.

I'm ready for this, and I don't just mean the ride.

Chapter Three

I can see the draw of riding on a motorbike. The sense of freedom, the adrenaline, the speed. I hold on to Temper and smile the whole way, glancing around and taking everything in. I'm sad to admit that it's been such a long time since I've done something new or ticked something off my bucket list, and that it took Temper coming here to get me to finally let loose.

When was the last time I smiled like this?

It's scary thinking of the person the last few months has made me, when I should be living my best life and enjoying every precious second of it.

When the bike comes to a stop, it's in front of our town's flashiest hotel. We don't have a five-star hotel here, but the mayor recently built a three-star, hoping it would attract more tourists.

It didn't, and now we have this new building that looks so out of place compared to the rest of the old town—a hotel the locals refuse to even look at.

Getting off the bike and removing my helmet, I arch my brow at him. "You're taking me to a hotel?" I don't know how to feel about this. Why would he bring me here? If he thinks I'm going to sleep with him, he has another think coming.

"Not exactly," he replies, grinning at me. "Have some faith, Abbie. You're safe with me."

Not exactly? I don't know what his plan is, and I don't even know if I should be here with him right now.

I need to trust him, or I need to leave.

"Okay," I reply, studying him. "I'm not going to sleep with you." Might as well get that out in the open right now.

His eyes widen. "Oh fuck, Abbie. I know. That's not what this is, all right? I promise." He shakes his head then mumbles, "I never thought how this would look to you, Jesus Christ."

Okay, so we're not here for sex, good to know.

We leave our helmets on his motorcycle, and I hold my new jacket in my hands as we enter. The place is empty, besides an older lady working at the desk.

"Is it ready?" he asks her.

Her face lights up when she sees us, probably happy to have something to do. I've seen her come into Franks a few times—Rita, her name is. "Yes, it's all ready for you, sir."

She hands him a key, and we both step into the elevator. He presses the button for the top floor, and we both head upward.

I glance at him. "This is my first time in this hotel."

"Good," he replies, lip twitching. "Then you won't know what to expect."

"I haven't known what to expect all night; I thought we'd be going to one of the local diners," I admit. "You know, like every other dinner date that happens in this town."

He chuckles. "You deserve more than ordinary. I finally get to take you out after all these years, you think I'm not going to put a little effort in? I mean, I didn't have much to work with here, but that doesn't mean I'm not going to try."

Ducking my head, I can't wipe the smile off my face. "That was cute."

"I don't think anyone has ever called me cute before," he muses, amusement in his tone.

People would probably be too scared to. Being with him here right now it's hard to believe he's this scary badass biker president, one they've even nicknamed Temper. I wonder when I will see that side of him.

"Maybe they're too scared to," I say out loud, just as the elevator doors open. We step into a beautiful foyer and through to a door on the right.

"Here we are," he comments, opening the door with a key card and gesturing for me to enter. The lights are all on as I step inside, my eyes widening as I take in the spread in front of me, right in the center of the luxurious suite, one I didn't even think this town was capable of.

"You got them to make a candlelit dinner for us?" I ask, eyeing the wine, the cheeses, dips, bread and olives.

"Well, I wanted something private, and different," he admits, closing the door and pulling out a chair for me. "They said they could make anything I want, so I thought we could start with this and then you could order whatever else you wanted." He watches me. "How did I do?"

"How did you do?" I repeat, smiling widely. I want to say that I've never really been on a proper date before, and that he's really setting the bar high, but I don't know if I want him to know that about me and how inexperienced I am just yet.

"Really well," I say, sitting down and waiting for him to do the same. Staring into his face in the candlelight,

I've never been happier that I took a chance and said yes to this date. "I appreciate the effort you went through."

He shrugs, like it was no big deal, and pours us some red wine. "So when do you think you'll be able to go back to college?"

"I'm not sure," I reply, accepting the glass. "Thank you."

"You're welcome."

"My mom had a stroke, and she has to take some medication now because of her heart. She's still resting for now, but they think she's going to be fine as long as she continues to take her meds. I don't know, she just doesn't need any stress right now, so I told her I will handle everything until she's stronger," I explain, lift the glass to my lips and take a sip.

"You're a good daughter," he says, nodding. "Putting your life on hold to take care of her."

"What's family for, right?" I reply with a small smile. "I mean, anyone in my position would have done it. Franks means a lot to her, and she means a lot to me. It's that simple. All I have is my mom and Ivy, and I'd do anything for them."

"Loyalty is one of the best traits that anyone can have," he says, studying me. "I'm not surprised at all though, you've always shown nothing but kindness to everyone around you. I also like to think I'm a good judge of character."

"I like to think I'm the same," I reply, glancing up at him through my lashes. I take one of the breadsticks and bite into it. "But I don't know if that's why I said no all the other times you asked me out, or why I finally said yes."

He laughs at that, a deep, musical sound. "You have nothing to worry about from me, Abbie."

"And other people?" I press, raising my brows.

He flashes his teeth. "I can't make any promises."

"They should have called you trouble instead of Temper," I mutter, helping myself to the food and serving it on my plate. "My mom would kill me if she knew I was here right now. She warned me to stay away from bikers."

He places his hand on his heart like he's offended. "Ah, come on. We're not all that bad."

"I know that," I agree, smirking. "But you're not all that good, either."

"You're smart," he replies, lip twitching. He's smart too, because he then changes the subject. "You should come and visit me sometime. This once or twice a year thing isn't going to cut it anymore."

"I'd love to do some traveling," I admit. "Even if it's just across a few states."

"Then do it. I'm sure Ivy could hold down the fort for a week or so," he says, brown eyes pinned on me.

This time it's me who changes the subject. "How is it being president?"

He drinks some of his wine. "Honestly? I wish Hammer was still here. I miss him every day, and it's hard trying to fill his shoes. But he trusted me, and I like to think I'm doing a good job."

"It must be a lot of pressure," I find myself saying. "I mean, you have to look after everyone, and make all of the decisions, right? That must be stressful sometimes."

"It can be, yes," he agrees, nodding. "It's not for everyone, that's for sure. But like you said before, there's nothing I won't do for my family, either."

We share a look.

I never thought I'd be sharing family values with someone like Temper, but he's right, his MC brothers are his family, and they have each other's backs just like I have Mom's and Ivy's.

"Why are you single?" I ask, tilting my head to the side and studying him. "Don't women throw themselves at you? I mean, I've seen a few of them trying to talk to you at Franks, but you always ignore them."

"I think I'm going to need another bottle," he jokes, dips a cracker in some cheese and thoughtfully chews before responding. "I'm just too busy with the MC, and I don't know, I did my fair share of sleeping around when I was younger, and it lost its appeal. Meaningless sex doesn't interest me anymore. I kind of just stick to myself these days, if I'm being honest. I enjoy my alone time, and my own company."

"So basically you're a grumpy old man set in your ways?" I tease.

I'm pretty sure he's not going without sex, but I don't know how to bring that up without sounding nosy.

"Something like that." He laughs, leaning back in his chair with a smile lingering on his full lips. "Plus it's hard to trust people these days, you know? And being who I am, I can only be around people that I trust completely. I don't know if you've noticed, but I'm a little bit rough around the edges. Not everyone can handle that."

"You clean up nicely," I blurt out, checking out his fresh shirt.

His expression stays the same, but those brown eyes smile, making me melt in my seat.

I don't know what I wanted out of tonight, but I didn't expect this, and I'm hoping that he kisses me before the night is over.

And if he doesn't, maybe I'll kiss him.

After all—right now is for living.

Chapter Four

We finish the grazing plate, and then end up ordering more food. We switch from wine to soda, and keep chatting into the night, moving right next to each other instead of on opposite sides of the table. We even put some music on, giving the hotel room quite the vibe.

"Ivy said you had to be home by twelve," Temper says, checking his watch. "It's eleven."

I roll my eyes. "I can be home whenever I want to. I'm a grown-ass woman." I pause, and then add, "But I should probably message her and let her know that I'm alive."

He smirks.

I send my sister a quick message and then glance around the suite. "Are you going to stay here tonight?"

"No, I'm going to head back to the clubhouse," he says, glancing down at his own phone.

"You have a clubhouse here and back in California?"

"This is the Nevada chapter's clubhouse," he explains to me. "So not ours exactly, but we're welcome there whenever we're in town. We're leaving first thing in the morning."

"Oh," I whisper. "So, I'll see you next year then?"

Quite the depressing thought, but what did I expect?

This date was an experience, and that's all it's ever going to be. I still don't regret coming tonight. If anything, I regret not saying yes to him the very first time he asked me out.

"Or you could come and visit me," he says, narrowing his gaze slightly. "Or you could even come with me tomorrow."

My eyes widen. "Yeah, I can't do that. Maybe I could come and visit sometime, but I can't just leave tomorrow with no warning. I have to work. And my mom."

He nods slowly. "I understand. I'll tell you what, give me your phone. I'm going to give you my number, and you message me, or call me."

"You chat on the phone?" I tease.

"Not unless it's an emergency," he replies, lip twitching. "But for you I'll make an exception. You call me if you ever need anything, you hear me? Anything. You need something, I got you."

Our eyes lock and connect.

This is the moment.

The acoustic version of "Power Over Me" by Dermot Kennedy plays, the powerful song setting the mood. He cups my cheek with his rough fingers, and my eyes flutter shut of their own accord, and I'm still, so still, just waiting. When his lips press against mine, I melt into him, tasting him gently at first, then I get a little bolder, exploring, my tongue brushing against his. I can feel my heart racing, the butterflies in my stomach out of control. This is *the* kiss.

Our instincts take over and soon I'm sitting on his lap, straddling him, his fingers in my hair and mine resting on his hard chest.

When we pull apart, our faces are still close together,

scanning each other's eyes. I lick my lips, still tasting him there, and feeling bold, I cup his stubbled cheek and press another soft kiss against his mouth.

"You're so beautiful," he whispers. "Your eyes, I can't look away from them."

I smile widely and rest my forehead against his. "Where have you been?"

"Asking you out every year and getting rejected," he murmurs, chuckling, and trails kisses down my neck. "I better get you home."

"Yeah, I guess so," I reply, moving back when I feel how hard he is. Clearing my throat, I slide off him, my cheeks heating a little.

He chuckles and says, "I might need a minute," making me blush even further. Trying to keep myself busy, I tidy up the table and put my shoes back on. Then we head back down on the elevator, this time so different from the last, the air so thick with sexual tension I don't even know where to look right now.

Licking my lips, I stare at the numbers of the floors, watching us get closer to the ground all while I can feel his brown eyes pinned on me. He says nothing, and does nothing, but I'm finding it hard to breathe, hard to not push him against the wall and kiss him once more.

I exhale as the door opens, and step out in front of him. He leaves the key card on the counter and walks out with me. Sliding the leather jacket back on, he hands me the helmet, staring at me. He opens his mouth to say something, but then closes it and stays quiet. I don't know what he wants to say, but if he's feeling the same as me—he doesn't want tonight to end.

It would be easy to walk away. I mean, we've only

had this night together, but these butterflies in my stomach and the way he makes me feel is confusing me.

No one has ever looked at me the way he looks at me.

It's both unnerving and all consuming.

"Better get you home," he mutters under his breath. "Where do you live?"

"Just around the corner from Franks," I say, and give the directions before hopping back on the bike behind him, and holding on to him once more. His phone rings before we ride off, and he says okay to whoever is on the line then hangs up.

"We have to make a stop first, if you don't mind," he says as he turns his head back.

"That's fine," I reply, kind of happy our night has been extended a little.

He revs the engine and off we go. I can't stop thinking about our kiss and how amazing it was. It wasn't awkward at all, which is surprising, especially with my lack of experience. I'm imagining him kissing me again, only to be pulled out of my daydream when he comes to a stop in front of two men. Behind them is a warehouse. Is this the clubhouse he was referring to?

Temper jumps off the bike and helps me down.

"Look what we have here," Renny calls out as he walks over to us, his brown eyes wide. "Hello, Abbie— how are you, sweetheart?"

"I'm good. Good to see you again, Renny," I say after my helmet comes off.

He eyes the two of us, a wide grin on his face.

"I'm going to kill you," Temper says to him, then looks towards Saint, who appears next. I wouldn't think I'd be on a first name basis with all these bikers, but after seeing them over the years, it's hard not to be. They're actually pretty friendly and seem like good guys. "What's this emergency you needed me for? Looks like the two of you are standing around and talking shit."

Two other men appear from inside the warehouse, men that I've never seen before. They are wearing different colors on their cuts, which makes me guess that they are a part of a different club.

"Stay here with her," Temper says to Saint, before bringing his gaze back to me. "I'll just be one second."

"Okay."

He walks toward the men, while I give my attention to Saint. "Never thought I'd see Temper taking a woman out on a date," he says, lip twitching.

"Never thought I'd be hanging out with bikers in my spare time," I fire back, making him laugh out loud. He keeps his eyes on Temper, as if making sure everything is okay, watching his back.

"Who are they?" I ask quietly.

"Acquaintances, I guess you could say," he replies, narrowing his blue eyes. "I didn't realize Temper was still with you, or I wouldn't have asked him to come here."

"We were just on our way home," I say, then quickly correct myself. "I mean, he was dropping me back at my house. I don't mind if he has to make a stop for... uh, work, or whatever."

Don't need anyone to think that I was about to take him home.

Saint chuckles under his breath. "Work. You're cute, you know that? All innocent and shit."

"I'm not inno—"

Yelling draws my attention back to Temper and the

men he was speaking to, my eyes widening as four men appear from nowhere, dressed in all black, guns in their hands. What the hell? Panic starts to fill me—I have no idea how this is going to play out.

Saint grabs me by the arm and quickly leads me to a car, opening the door and all but shoving me inside. "Stay in here and stay low."

He runs off just as I hear gunshots go off. Lifting my head, I can't help but look through the window, my eyes darting around for Temper. He starts to chase the men, but Renny calls his name, so he stops and turns back. My eyes then move to Renny, who is standing there with a gun in his hand, one of the men on the ground by his feet.

He isn't moving.

Renny's gun is still pointed at his body.

There's blood, a lot of blood.

Temper walks over to him, kneels down and checks the man's pulse at his neck. My eyes go back to Renny, who is now looking at the gun in his hand, still as a statue.

Oh my God.

The man doesn't move, and Temper looks up at Renny, shaking his head, and he then brings his eyes to the car I'm in.

To me.

I duck my head back down, crouched on the floor, staying hidden.

Holy crap. I just witnessed a murder.

Wrapping my arms around myself, I wonder how the fuck tonight turned into this. I had the perfect date with Temper, and now a quick stop on the way home has turned into me witnessing something I never should have seen.

As if reading my thoughts, Temper comes over to the car, opening the door and sitting next to me. "Fuck," he whispers, clenching his teeth, and I sit properly on the seat, staring straight ahead.

"Who were those men?" I ask, feeling numb at this point, and not knowing what to do or say. Maybe I'm going into shock, I don't know.

"I don't know," he admits, staring straight ahead. "We've never seen them before, but they obviously wanted us all dead. If Renny didn't have that gun on him, we probably wouldn't be here right now."

"Did Renny kill him?" I dare ask.

Temper stays silent, and then whispers, "I should have taken you home first. I shouldn't have stopped. I just didn't think…" He trails off. "We've never had any problems here, with anyone."

"Temper—"

He slams his fists against the back of the driver's seat. "Fuck!"

"Can you take me home now, please?" I say, swallowing hard. I just want this night to be over. In fact, I'm going to pretend anything after our date never happened.

I could have died tonight.

What if I was accidentally shot? If I was standing somewhere else when the guns went off? What if it was me lying there on the ground, in a pool of my own blood?

"He hasn't moved. He's dead," I announce, shaking my head. I stare at the man, whose light hair is covered in blood. "Oh my God, he's dead."

Temper finally brings his gaze to me, studying me. I don't like the look in his eyes—it's a look I've never seen before from him, almost a detached look of con-centration. He then glances outside, I'm assuming at Renny or Saint, and gives a slight nod.

"Come on, I'll take you home," he says, sighing. "And for what it's worth, Abbie. I'm sorry. I'm so fuckin' sorry."

I follow him out of the car, toward his motorcycle.

I thought he was saying sorry for what I had wit-nessed tonight, but when I'm grabbed from behind with a hand covering my mouth, I know that he was only apologizing for what's to come.

Chapter Five

With my hands and feet tied in front of me, rope around my mouth like a gag, I stare out the window and wonder how the fuck I'm going to escape. I'm guessing it's because I'm now a witness to a murder their MC committed. The thing is, though, I wouldn't have said anything. I saw what happened, those men came at them with guns, so it wasn't like they killed some innocent person, but that doesn't excuse anything.

Temper isn't even in this car; he's riding his motorcycle while I'm stuck with two men by the names of Chains and Crow. I've seen them in Franks, but only in the last year or so—they must be new. Crow is driving, while Chains is in the back, probably to make sure I don't try anything.

"I'll take the rope off and give you some water. Just don't scream, or I'm going to stop and put you in the trunk," he warns me, his dark, menacing eyes telling me that he's not bluffing.

I nod once, and he removes the rope, watching me carefully. Chains brings a bottle of water to my lips and lets me have a few sips. "You want any more?" he asks.

I shake my head. "Where are we going? I need to speak to Temper."

Maybe if I can just explain that I'm not going to say anything, maybe he will let me go. There's no need for any of this. My mom and my sister will be so worried about me if I don't come home. Even though I texted Ivy that everything was going great, if I'm not there when she wakes up she's going to know that something is wrong. It's not like me to not check in with her, especially when she knows who I was going on a date with.

He points out the window at Temper on his bike. "He's a little busy at the moment."

"Everything is going to be fine, Abbie," Crow promises from the front. "We just need to sort out some shit, and we need to know that you aren't going to go running to the cops in the meantime."

Finally, someone gives it to me straight, which I appreciate.

"I'm not going to go to the cops, okay?" I tell them. "If Temper actually let me speak before he kidnapped me, I would have told him that."

"We can't take that chance," Chains comments from beside me. "You aren't going to be hurt in any way, and when this is all done with, then you can go back home."

"All done with how? That man isn't going to magically come back to life," I snap, regretting my words as soon as they leave my lips. No point pointing out to them that there is no way out of this. What's done is done, and yes, I saw what happened, and nothing is going to change that, but I meant what I said—I have no intention of getting myself involved in this in any way.

"How do you know we didn't take him to the hospital? He could be alive." Chains smirks. "You don't know what happened."

"It wasn't looking good for him," I mutter, shifting on the seat. "And if he's fine, then why am I here?"

"Maybe we just want to make sure that you're safe. How do we know those men aren't going to come after you next? They saw you. And they know what *you* saw. They know you saw what they looked like."

Exhaling deeply, I stretch my neck from side to side before replying, "I think you're grasping at straws here, but whatever. Whether he's alive or dead, I just want to mind my business and pretend all of this never happened. I wanted a little excitement in my life, but this is just a joke now."

Chains points to the sign to the left of us. "You're leaving the state, I'm sure that's exciting for you. Temper mentioned you haven't really been anywhere."

"Well, how kind of you all to take me traveling," I reply in a dry tone, scowling in his direction. "You're a real asshole, you know that?"

"He does," Crow says from the front. "I told you that I should have sat with her. Your bedside manner needs some fuckin' work."

"So you're saying there's a good way to kidnap a woman?" Chains fires back, crossing his arms over his chest. "I'm sorry, but this is the first time I've been in this situation."

Leaning my head back, I close my eyes. *Think, Abbie, think.*

"I need to pee," I announce.

Maybe if I can get away from them, I can call Ivy to come pick me up, and Mom won't even have to know anything that has happened. It will save me from her "I told you so" speech, which I'm not looking forward to.

She told me to stay away from the bikers, and I didn't listen, because Temper was too much of a temptation.

"I'll stop at the next gas station," Crow says. He seems nicer than Chains, and definitely has a kinder disposition.

"Thank you."

"Don't even think of trying anything," Chains says, watching me from the corner of his eye. "If you get away, Temper will actually fuckin' kill me, and we don't need another death happening today."

"So he did die," I state, taking a deep breath. "I don't know how I got dragged into this. My life was so simple before I went on this date with Temper."

And now I understand why he doesn't date. Maybe this is his life and this shit just follows him around all the time. I feel a dash of sympathy for him, but he chose this life, and I guess this is the downside to it. Renny has only ever been polite and kind to me, and I had no idea he could be capable of what I saw today, which only shows how naïve I am. I know he was protecting himself and his brothers, but this whole incident has just made me regret ever looking in Temper's direction. He's not even here right now, making sure that I'm okay. Instead he's on his bike, probably enjoying his life while I'm fucking tied up here with his men.

This wasn't how I ever pictured him tying me up would be. I was imagining a little more consent, and a lot more fun.

Anger fills me. He's the president, so he could have handled this situation any way he wanted, and this is his best option? He's either a complete idiot or he just panicked and did what he could to temporarily fix the situation—at my expense, of course.

Either way, I think it's safe to say my dating life with any type of bikers is well and truly done with.

"He's a good man," Crow says, sticking up for his leader. "Don't judge him by what happened tonight. He's doing the best he can in a fucked-up situation none of us saw coming."

"We didn't see the date with you coming either," Chains mutters, running his hand through his dark hair. "I don't think he's ever been on a date since I joined the MC."

"I think we have bigger problems right now," I reply, scowling and lifting up my tied hands. "Well, at least I do."

Crow, the bastard, can't help but laugh out loud. "I like you, Abbie."

"Wish the feeling was mutual," I reply, gritting my teeth. "What are you guys going to do when my sister reports me missing and the cops come after you? Everyone saw me leaving with Temper, and I'm sure that your clubhouse isn't that hard to find."

"What happens next is up to Temper," Chains replies, checking a text message on his phone. "I'm sure he has a plan, or at least he will come up with one."

Just fucking great.

And I'm sure they're right. Temper didn't become president by default; he was chosen because he's obviously intelligent, crafty, and knows how to strategize and fix things when they go wrong.

"We can stop here," Crow says, pulling into a gas station. "But Abbie, if you try anything, it's not going to end well." He gives me a look that tells me he means business. When I nod, he says, "Chains, untie her."

Come on. They can't expect me to not try anything.

They've fucking taken me without my consent, and I don't care how they try to justify that, but it's not okay. They can try the whole "it's for my best interest and safety" bit all they want, but I'm a grown woman and I should be the one making decisions for myself, no one else.

I wait patiently as he unties my feet first, and then my hands. I don't miss Temper's bike pulling in next to us, and this is the first time I'm going to face him since the whole kidnapping spiel.

I'm not going to lie, I'm scared, I'm numb, but more than anything, I'm fucking angry.

I trusted him, I let him in, and this is what I get.

I don't know why I'm so surprised, given who he is, but I am. I thought Temper and I had a connection. I don't know, my gut instinct was telling me that I could trust him, which just goes to show I have zero common sense and should probably never be let out alone again.

Temper opens my car door and stares down at me, those brown eyes I was melting into only a few hours ago now cold and emotionless.

What a talent he has, to be able to turn his feelings off and on like a faucet.

"Come on," he says, offering me his hand. "I'll walk you in."

His tone, the one I was getting used to, is no longer gentle. Now it's strictly business, and it pisses me off even further.

I ignore his hand and stand up of my own accord. "How kind of you."

He gently holds on to my upper arm and leads me inside, straight to the restroom before I can even get a chance to look around. Opening the door to the female toilets, he says, "You have three minutes."

"Great," I reply, slamming the door in his face.

Turning around, I scan the bathroom looking for an escape route. There's a window above the sinks, but I'm not sure if I'm going to be able to fit through it… Fuck it, I have nothing to lose at this point and I'm going to do everything I can to get away.

Standing up on the counter, I slowly open the window, attempting not to make a noise. Once it's fully open, I move forward and try to push myself through it, my body half dangling out, my hips stuck.

"Fuck," I whisper, swiveling my body, my legs flopping around behind me.

If Temper walks in right now…

Realizing this plan isn't going to work, I attempt to push my body back down, but that doesn't seem to work either.

I'm stuck.

In the gas station window, trying to escape from my crush slash captor.

Shit like this could only happen to me.

Chapter Six

I hear the door open, and then…laughter. The booming sound makes me clench my fists and want to yell at him.

"Quite the view from here," he says, and I know he's staring at my ass, which is perched up in the air waiting for someone to save it. Thank God I didn't wear a dress tonight.

"Can you just…not give me any shit and help me down?" I call out, pursing my lips, wiggling, still trying to get free. "This isn't exactly the most comfortable position I've ever been in."

Understatement of the year.

Big hands cup my hips and I suck my stomach in as he gently pulls me back down on the counter.

"You don't need to try to escape me, Abbie. I'm not going to let anything happen to you, all right? You just need to trust me right now, and let me fix what has happened." His tone is back to being gentle, like he's letting himself open up again. The stoic, emotionless Temper gone once more.

Oh, so now he's trying to be nice. Did he realize the big bad captor thing wasn't working on me, so he's trying a different tactic?

"You kidnapped me," I state, sitting down on the

counter and staring daggers at him. "And you're acting like I'm supposed to be okay with this! That is *not*
okay, Temper. I don't care who you are. And you're not
my president, so guess what? I don't have to listen to
you. As far as I'm concerned, you're an asshole, and
going on that date with you was the biggest mistake of
my life. Now why don't you let me go before the cops
start looking for you, and we can just call it a day?"

He looks me dead in the eye, and I don't miss the
regret and sadness there. "I should have taken you
straight home. But I didn't. I wanted to stretch out our
fuckin' date as much as I could and now it's landed
us here, in this messed-up situation. But I'm trying to
handle it, okay? I couldn't just leave you back there,
knowing what you saw, and knowing those men also
saw you."

In some fucked-up way, even though it's the same
thing Chains and Crow said to me in the car, I can see
it from his side and get where he's coming from. He had
seconds to think about what to do and he made this decision. However, in my world, kidnapping someone is
not the appropriate answer. To him, this seems almost
normal, and I'm not okay with that.

He thinks he can do whatever the hell he wants, and
somehow justifies it to himself.

It's fucked.

"You tied me up," I say, scanning his gaze. "And
left me in a car with men I don't know. None of these
things are normal."

He sighs. "You're right. I made the wrong call. But
I can't go back and fix what happened."

I appreciate his honesty and admitting fault, but it
doesn't change anything. "I need to call my sister and

let her know I'm okay. Can you at least let me do that? She's going to be worried sick."

He studies me. "And what are you going to tell your sister?"

Looking down at my hands, I say, "That I'm okay and not to worry."

"More like tell her where you are and to call the cops," he replies in a dry tone, pulling me off the counter and leads me back outside.

After my first botched attempt at an escape, and with nothing to lose, I decide to try once more. I look toward the gas station attendant and call out for help.

"Help me! Call the police! He kidnapped me!" I scream as he simply looks at Temper and says, "See you next time."

My jaw drops open and I stop short, Temper nearly colliding with me. I turn toward him. "Seriously? What, you have gas attendants on your payroll? What kind of bullshit operation is this?"

"He looks the other way, we bring him business. It's a business transaction," Temper replies, his cheerful tone making me want to scream.

"You're an asshole!" I call out.

I don't know who I'm speaking to, because they are all assholes, each and every one of them.

"You want me to sit in the car with you?" Temper continues. "You said you were pissed that I left you in there with strangers. I don't usually let anyone ride my bike, but I guess for you I can make an exception."

He's clearly not right in the head.

I tell him as much. "There's something seriously wrong with you. Ride your bike—it's basically been your girlfriend for all of your life, so I wouldn't want to make her jealous."

The men don't laugh, but I can tell that they want to, especially Crow, whose expressions are very open. I don't miss his lip twitching or the fact that he looks away to try to compose himself.

Temper makes a noise in the back of his throat. I can tell I'm frustrating him, but what does he expect. Still, he's gentle with me as he helps me back into my prison, and sits in the back with me, letting Chains ride his pride and joy.

"You can message your sister," he says after several minutes of tense silence. "Just let her know that you're fine, you've gone on a trip for a few days and will be home soon."

My eyes widen. "And wouldn't that just be so convenient for you. I'm not going to lie to my sister, no way in hell."

The bastard slides my phone out from his jeans pocket. "Well, good thing I already sent her that exact message then."

I see red.

I'm not a violent person, but my hands lash out at him, hitting him on his chest, and trying to push him away from me, trying to hurt him, just anything to make him feel even a fraction of what I'm feeling right now. How dare he do this to me? How dare he message my sister, making her think everything is okay and that I'm being irresponsible by taking a last-second break with a biker I went on one date with? I don't know if she's going to buy the story or not, but that's not the point. He's a controlling, manipulative asshole and he doesn't care who he has to step on to protect his beloved club of criminals.

He holds my wrists, and I know he's regretting not retying me right now. I know it's useless and I'm just wasting my energy. I almost want to apologize for my outburst, but I'm not going to.

He doesn't deserve to hear an apology from me.

"I hate you," I whisper to him, then glance out the window.

Maybe he's telling the truth. Maybe it will all be fine and he will let me go back home once all of this shit is sorted. When he knows that the murder is covered up, or the men who tried to kill them are no longer a threat. I don't really know what options I have.

I could continue to try to escape. Stay on my toes and use every chance I get to get away.

Or I could just play a waiting game, but that would mean trusting him, and he hasn't quite shown me that he deserves my trust.

How am I supposed to trust his word now?

I don't even want to give him the satisfaction of giving in and making this easy on him. He probably thought I'd give him no trouble. Poor innocent little Abbie, who has never even left her home state before. I can only imagine the picture of myself that I've painted. And I might not be cultured or worldly, but I'm not weak. And I'm not someone who can be easily manipulated.

Apparently I am someone who can be kidnapped and not be able to escape, though.

Crow decides that turning up the music a little is going to save the atmosphere, Ed Sheeran filling the car. Temper runs his hand over his bald head and stays silent, but I can see his mind working through his sharp eyes.

Always thinking, planning, and strategizing.

It must be exhausting. Good. I hope he falls asleep. Maybe I can jump out of the car. Then I look outside, realizing Crow is driving pretty fast and I'd probably kill myself or get run over if I attempted that.

"Do you have an idea when am I going to be able to go home?" I ask Temper, exhaling deeply, all the anger leaving my body.

"I don't know," he replies, turning to me. "A week, maybe two. I can't say. But I can promise you that I will take you back home, safe and sound, after all of this blows over."

I glance out at the highway, leading me somewhere new. I could look at this as an adventure, as an escape. I still feel guilty leaving Ivy to look after Mom and Franks, but it's not like I chose this.

"What did Ivy reply to the message?" I ask, pursing my lips.

He pulls out my phone and reads the message out loud to me.

Ivy: Are you fucking crazy? Are you sure you're okay? Where are you going exactly? What do I tell Mom?

Ivy: ABBIE?!?!?

He hands me back my phone. "I'm trusting you right now and giving this back. But I think we both know it's in both of our best interests if you wait until this is all over before you head back home."

Squeezing my phone in my hands, I consider his

words. I don't want to bring any trouble around Mom or Ivy, but would whoever they are really come after me? They did see me standing there, and they know what I witnessed, but I'm pretty sure I'm more of a liability for the Knights than the men who tried to kill them.

But do I really want to take the chance? While I don't think those men care anything about me, I can't risk it. I live in a small town and Franks is one of the main places, so if they went there, they could figure out it was me. There are pictures of me throughout the bar—it's part of the family décor my mother likes to use.

I make a decision in that moment. "Okay," I say to him, nodding.

I type back to Ivy, answering all her questions, and making up excuses for why I'm not coming home.

I should have been more careful about what I wished for.

I wanted a change in my life, and I guess for now, I got it.

Chapter Seven

We continue driving through the night and as the sun starts to rise. I'm not sure where they live in California, but it's been at least four hours of driving.

California is everything I imagined it would be, just like I've seen on TV. I can't help but take everything in and enjoy the change in scenery, not that I'd ever admit that, though. It's definitely greener than Nevada, and much more densely populated.

When we pull up to our destination, which I am assuming is the clubhouse, there's a woman getting out of her car. She's beautiful, with long, thick, dark hair. "Who is that?" I ask Temper.

"Izzy," he replies, his shoulder touching mine. "Renny's old lady."

Renny has an old lady? "Oh," I whisper, brow furrowing. I move away from Temper so we're no longer touching. "Are you guys going to tell her what happened?"

"No," Temper says quickly, and when I turn back to him, his eyes are narrowed on me. "And neither are you. It's up to Renny what he does or does not tell her—that's not our business."

"How is that not our business? We were all there, I

was there, and now I'm here because of it. How are you going to explain me being here exactly?" I ask, shaking my head. "I thought that the MC were all honest and loyal with each other."

"We are," he replies, scowling at my judgment. "But the women aren't members, are they?"

My eyes narrow. "So what? The women aren't on the same level as the men? No gender equality through those clubhouse doors? So you lie to your women? I'm so glad I'm seeing all this before anything else happened between us."

"I'm going to take this moment to leave," Crow declares from the front, making a quick escape. I actually forgot Crow was even here.

"What Renny tells Izzy is up to Renny. That's his business, just like what I tell you is my business," he says, jaw tight. "Come on, you must be hungry. Let's get you fed and showered."

"The only thing I want from you is to leave me alone."

I open the door and step out, crossing my arms over my chest. Izzy notices me straight away and tilts her head to the side as if confused. "Who is that?" I hear her ask Renny.

"Temper's woman," he explains, shrugging like it's no big deal.

"Temper doesn't have a woman," she says, wrinkling her nose. She then locks eyes with me and waves, closing the space between us. "Hello, I'm Izzy," she says with a smile, offering me her hand.

"Abbie," I say, giving her a forced smile in return. "And I'm not Temper's woman."

I hear the man in question sigh from behind me.

"I see," she replies, looking over my head. "Nice to have you all home. I'm looking forward to hearing this story."

"Can you take her in?" Temper asks her, clearing his throat. "And give her whatever she needs."

"Of course," Izzy says, brow furrowing. "Come on, let's get you inside."

I follow her but can't help but turn around to look at Temper, seeing him talk closely with Renny, probably preparing their smorgasbord of lies. I flip him the bird when our eyes catch, his unimpressed expression worth it.

"Would you like something to eat?" Izzy asks, opening the door and letting me in. "I'll give you a quick tour as we walk through."

The clubhouse isn't what I had imagined a bunch of bikers to live in. It's extremely neat, with no clutter for one, and from the inside looks like a comfortable home anyone could easily live in.

"I'd love something to eat," I admit to her as we step into the kitchen. I'd never tell Temper, but I'm starving. "So do you live here?"

"I actually live down the road," she explains, opening the fridge and scanning the contents. "But I spend a lot of my time here with Renny. There's last night's pizza. Or I can order you something in if you like?"

"Pizza sounds great," I tell her, my tummy rumbling. She heats us both some in the microwave, and we sit down at the table.

"So, you're here with Temper but you're not his woman?" she asks, eyes going wide. "You don't have to answer," she continues, noticing the scowl on my face. "I'm just wondering what the hell is going on here because I've never seen Temper give any woman the time of day before. And you don't seem like you want to be here right now, but you're not running, so what's the deal?"

I have no idea how to answer her questions without giving the whole situation away, but I don't want to lie to her. She seems nice, and I don't think she's going to let this go until she gets to the bottom of it.

"I went on one date with him," I admit. "Which was last night. But no, we aren't together or anything like that."

She arches her brow, silently begging me to continue.

"Some shit went down last night," I end up saying, and lick my suddenly dry lips. "And I happened to be there, and then Temper wasn't sure if I'd be safe staying there or not, so he made me come here until it all blows over. So no, I don't want to be here, but I don't want to risk my family getting hurt if I head back home either."

There. The truth, but I left out the part about her man killing someone, because apparently that's not my business to tell her that.

"He made you come here?" she asks, eyes narrowing as she leans forward. "Like as in against your will?" She takes the pizza out of the microwave and hands me a plate with a slice.

I shrug and pick up my piece of pizza. "I definitely didn't choose to be tied up and thrown into a car with random men."

Izzy's eyes widen and her mouth slips open. "Are you fucking kidding me? Renny!" she yells out, standing up and storming out of the kitchen.

Oops. Temper said not to tell her about what Renny

did, but he never said I couldn't tell her the truth about how I got here.

I hope she yells at Temper, too.

I finish the piece of pizza before she returns with Renny at her side. "You can't just kidnap a woman! What the hell were you guys thinking? You guys honestly can't be left alone, can you? What is wrong with you all?"

She continues ranting at him, all while he gives me a look that clearly says *thanks a lot for that, Abbie*.

I shrug again. It's the truth, so I shouldn't feel guilty about getting him in trouble with his missus. At least she's not like them, and clearly has a conscience and morals.

"You must have been terrified," she says, sitting back down and studying me. "You are safe, though, and you have my word on that, okay? No one is going to hurt you here."

Temper told me as much, and I do believe him, but it's nice to be reassured by her and to feel like I have someone on my side. "Thank you."

"You'll need clothes and toiletries," she says, glancing up at Renny. "I don't know how the hell I'm supposed to make what you guys have done to her better, but I'm going to try. I'm taking her shopping. And I'm using your credit card."

My lip twitches.

"You can use Temper's credit card," Renny fires back, smirking. "Max it out, he won't even care if it's all for her."

Izzy's eyebrows raise in surprise. She looks back at me, a contemplative expression on her face, her pretty green eyes working. "Do you want to shower and sleep first? We can go later if you're tired."

"A shower sounds great, but I'm not going to have anything to wear after," I think out loud. And there's no way I could fit into her much smaller-sized clothes. "So maybe we should go grab a few things first."

"Sounds good," she replies, still scowling at Renny.

I use the bathroom and wash my face, trying to make myself look a little more decent, while Izzy organizes our trip. I'm not at all surprised when Crow is waiting by the car.

"More babysitting?" I say in greeting.

"Aw, come on, don't be like that. I'm just coming along to give my opinion on the latest fashions," he fires back, opening the door for me. "And to get something to eat—I'm starving."

Crow drives, and Izzy sits with me in the back seat. "You have really pretty eyes, you know that?" she says to me. "They are so unique."

"Thank you. I used to hate them," I explain. "I was teased in school growing up, because no one accepted anything that was different."

And I was always different.

"People are assholes," she replies, making me grin. "But honestly, they are stunning. I can see why you caught Temper's eye."

I can feel my cheeks start to heat. "I'm so out of my element," I quietly admit.

She squeezes my hand. "I've got you. Don't even worry about it. I think you have more power than you know you have in this situation."

It doesn't feel that way at all, but it's nice to hear.

Crow stops at a mall bigger than I've ever seen in person, and walks behind us, letting us lead the way.

"This place is insane," I tell Izzy, eyes as wide as saucers. I spot a store with beautiful clothing in the windows. "Can we go in there?"

"Yeah, of course. We can go anywhere you want to," she says, grinning.

I pick up two pairs of jeans, three tops, a dress and some pajamas, trying everything on first and making sure it all fits. I don't want to spend too much of Temper's money, but it's not like I have my purse on me. He gave me back my phone, but not my handbag, so I couldn't even pay for any of it if I wanted to. When I step out of the change room, Izzy is standing there with a whole pile of items in her hand.

"Do you like any of these? This store has really nice shit," she says, setting the clothes down on the table.

"I don't want to spend too much of his money," I tell her, eying the items she chose. "Oh wow, that dress is amazing."

Izzy comes closer to me and says, "He kidnapped you. Don't feel bad spending his money. Consider it reimbursement for what he has put you through."

"I like you," I state.

She grins evilly. "I like you, too."

We leave the store with a bill of $1200, and then continue on to pick up some toiletries, bras and underwear and another pair of shoes.

Temper then even treats me, Izzy and Crow to a steak for lunch. "I love this place," I admit to them both. "There's so many options. Back home we have one small Walmart, and that's about it." And they never have many clothing options, so most of my shopping is done online.

"Do you want to go anywhere else?" Izzy asks me, smiling at my excitement. "We can go and see a movie, or do some sightseeing? I'm sure Temper won't mind as long as you're safe."

Crow flashes me a look and picks up his phone to call and ask the boss himself. "Izzy wants to take Abbie sightseeing, and God knows where else. Is that all good?" He pauses, and then goes, "Yep, okay. Bye."

He glances up at us. "Looks like today we are your tour guides."

Sounds interesting.

Chapter Eight

Hands full of bags, we step back into the clubhouse. After having such an amazing day with Izzy and Crow, playing tourist and visiting all the sights—Grauman's Chinese Theater with the hand and footprints in the cement, Beverly Hills, the Santa Monica Pier—I'm exhausted, but I feel…exhilarated. I've wanted to travel for so long and just experience something new, but I never got the chance, and now it's taken something as crazy as the situation I'm in to get me there. I can be bitter about this whole thing or I can make the most out of it, and I think I definitely did that today. Izzy and I get along really well, and it's weird to think that I've made a friend out of all of this.

I don't know how this is my life, but here we are.

Temper isn't at the clubhouse when I get there, which is kind of a relief. It gives me time to have a shower, get changed and feel human again. Izzy shows me to my temporary room and makes me feel at home.

"We're going to order in some Chinese tonight, and you'll get to meet Skylar. She's the best. She's with Saint, and her stepdad was Hammer, our old president," she explains, and helps me pack away all of my new stuff into the closet. "You'll love her. We're going to have to buy you a suitcase so you can take all of this stuff home."

"Oh no, I guess that means another trip back to the mall," I reply with a grin. "If Temper gives me back my purse that would be great, though, because I don't want to rely on anyone else paying for shit for me."

"Yeah, that would be annoying," she agrees, frowning. "I swear, sometimes men just don't think. Even if making him pay is great revenge for him bringing you here." She gives me a wink.

"At least I got my phone back," I say, checking my messages from Ivy. "I feel like a teenager who has gotten in trouble and got her shit confiscated."

Izzy laughs softly. "I'd be so fucking angry. You're handling all of this so well. We're going to have fun, though. I'll make sure of it."

"I had fun with you today," I admit, smiling. "Thank you for taking me under your wing. I can only imagine how it would have been if you weren't here when we pulled in. I probably would have been thrown into a dungeon with some bread and water."

She laughs again, just as Temper steps into the room, pushing the slightly ajar door open and taking us both in. "Have a fun day?" he asks me, eying the bags on the floor. "It looks like you did."

"I made the most of it," I reply, lifting my chin. "Thanks to Izzy and Crow."

"Good," he replies, looking at Izzy. "Can I speak to Abbie alone, please?"

"Sure," Izzy says, moving to the door. "I'll be in the kitchen if you need me."

"Why is she going to need you?" he asks her, frowning. "We're just going to have a chat."

"I don't know, emotional support," Izzy calls out as she closes the door.

Temper turns to me. "Great, a few hours with her and you've turned her against me."

"You're the president," I say, brow furrowing. "I don't think anyone can do anything other than like you."

He sits down on my bed and sighs. "I appreciate you not giving them a hard time today. I wasn't sure if they were going to catch you stuck in any windows or not."

"Ha ha, very funny," I grumble, crossing my arms over my chest. "You had to bring that up, didn't you? And no, they were both lovely, and took the time to show me around. It was really nice, actually. And I feel bad that we used your card but you kind of took mine away from me, so I didn't really have any options."

"You can have it back. I completely forgot; it's still in the glove box in the car," he admits. "But you can use my card. What's mine is yours. You have no reason to feel bad. It's the least that I can do."

"Izzy said something similar."

"Of course she did," he mutters, running his hand over his head. "Come on, I want to officially introduce you to all of my men."

"Okay." I like that he's trying to make me feel welcome here, but it's hard to forget how I got here in the first place. If I was here under different circumstances, like I came to visit him, it would be so very different, and I know I would have loved every minute of being here.

When I'm about to move past him, he stops me with a hand on my shoulder and steps around me so we're facing each other. Cupping my cheek, he looks deeply into my eyes. "I'm sorry for how I handled everything, but I panicked and I went into president mode, and I did whatever I had to do to keep everyone safe at the time. I know that I fucked up, though, and I'm sorry, okay?"

"You did fuck up," I agree, brow furrowing. "I think what concerns me the most is that you can just make these decisions for everyone without caring what they might think or feel."

"It's my job to make these decisions," he fires back, frowning. "And I have everyone to think about, not just me or you."

I'm assuming he means he had to also think about Renny, because if I went to the cops, he would be doing time behind bars, and no one wants that. It's just a really shitty situation, and unfortunately, I drew the short stick with the whole thing.

"I get it, I do," I say.

"But?"

But… I guess I'm holding a grudge over the kidnapping thing and it's going to take me some time to trust him again. If I ever do trust him again.

"But I'm still angry. And I'm allowed to be. You didn't even talk to me to give me any choices at all, and you've shown me a side of you that I don't like. Come on, let's go," I say, walking out the door.

He stays silent after my rant, and so do I. I really like Izzy and Crow and it's not anyone else's fault that I'm here, so I'm not going to make a scene.

Izzy is where she said she would be, in the kitchen with Renny standing behind her, his arms wrapped around her. We get some beers and vodka and head outside, Temper lighting a bonfire in the backyard. People soon arrive, amongst them Izzy's sister Ariel with Trade, who I find out is Temper's younger brother, and Saint's girlfriend, Skylar, who I warm to instantly.

"Izzy told me what happened," Skylar says, her beautiful red hair falling over her sharp green eyes. "Are you doing okay?"

I nod. "I am. And I spoke to my sister and she's holding down the fort, so I don't need to feel too guilty."

Or at least I can try. Ivy is extremely confused about my actions, but she's covered for me with Mom, and work. I'm so lucky to have her. She said I better call her with a proper explanation and that she needs to hear my voice, so I told her I'd be in touch tonight before bed.

"If there's anything I can do, let me know," Skylar says, reaching out and touching my shoulder. "I live here, too, so I'm always around, all right?"

"Thanks," I say, smiling. "Everyone has been nothing but nice since I got here." Which is kind of weird when you consider the situation.

"And who do we have here?" a newcomer asks, grinning as he sits down. He offers me his hand. "I'm Dee."

"Abbie."

"I've heard all about you," he replies, grabbing a beer off the table. "It's a shame I didn't go on this run—it looks like I've missed out on all of the fun."

"I don't know if I would call what happened fun," I reply in a dry tone. "More like traumatizing."

In fact, I've been trying to block it out. I've never seen anyone die before, and I think I'm just in denial about the whole thing.

Dee ducks his head. "I meant the whole 'Temper going on a date for the first time since I've known him' thing."

"Oh," I reply, wincing. He hands me a beer, and I accept it. We clink them together just as Temper sits down on my other side.

"Izzy has to work tomorrow, so I'm going to take you to L.A. to explore the city," he says, lifting his glass to his lips. "So if there's anything in particular you want to do or see, let me know."

"Is there no one else who can take me?" I ask, scratching the label off the beer bottle. "What's Crow doing?"

"He's busy." Temper scowls, jaw going tight.

"Renny?"

"Also busy," he fires back.

"Chains?" I ask, wrinkling my nose, because truth be told, I can't imagine him being good company.

"Really?" he replies, eyes narrowing. "I'm taking you, and that's that."

"Fine. I'll do a little research and see what else L.A. has to offer," I grumble. I know there's plenty of eateries I've been wanting to try, so I should slowly tick them off my list. When I get back home, who knows when I'm going to be able to leave again?

"Good," he replies, studying me. "When are you going to forgive me?"

"I don't know, what's the going time to hold a grudge on kidnapping?" I ask, arching my brow. "Probably twenty-five to life."

The same sentence he would probably get if I went to the police.

Okay, I'm exaggerating, but still.

Temper surprises me by laughing. "Fuckin' hell, what am I going to do with you?"

"Food is here!" Crow calls out, hands full of bags full of containers. Skylar helps him set it all out, and we all grab some plates and cutlery and dig in. Trade pretends to steal Izzy's prawn crackers, so she throws one at him.

Watching all of them interact, it's clear to see that they are really just one big, happy family, and somehow they just make it work. I can see how much they all care for each other, and Temper wanting to protect Renny is understandable. I feel like they'd always have each other's backs no matter what the other did, and no matter how bad it was.

I guess murdering someone would top that list.

"I love honey chicken," I say and chew one of the delicious round balls. "This food seriously beats our Chinese restaurant back home."

"You haven't seen anything yet," Izzy says, eyes bright. "There's so many places you need to go to before you leave. Especially because you're a foodie. The options are endless."

Excitement fills me. "Temper said he's taking me around tomorrow because you're working, so tell me where you think I should go for lunch."

"I'm working?" she replies, sounding confused, then looks over at Temper before bringing her gaze back to me. "Oh yeah. I have some work to do tomorrow."

"What do you do for work?" I ask, realizing that I have no idea.

"I'm a graphic designer," she explains. "And I work for myself, so it's super flexible. Temper said that you work in your family's bar back home?"

"Yeah, Franks." I nod. "I was in college, but I had to put it on hold to help my mom with the bar and restaurant. It's just me, her and my little sister."

"Franks? Why does that sound familiar?" I can tell she's giving that deep thought. "Oh my God, is it on the way home from Vegas? Pictures all around so it sort of feels like you're in someone's house?"

I turn red. Mom's décor strikes again. "Yup, that's us. You've stopped in before?"

She nodded. "Yeah, actually, when I first officially met Renny we did a road trip to Vegas together, and we stopped into there. Cute place. I remember the food being good."

"That sounds like an interesting story." I grin.

"You have no idea," she murmurs, rolling her eyes. "Ariel lived there at that time, and she was about to give birth. I needed a ride, and coincidentally, Renny was there to give me one. The rest is history."

"I feel like there's more to that story."

She laughs. "There is, and I'll tell you it from the beginning another time."

"Deal."

"You're a good daughter," she says, smiling at me. "I'm really close with my sister, too. Our mom passed away and our dad is an asshole, so we're all the family we have too. I mean, besides the MC, of course. They're definitely my family now."

"I can see that," I reply, glancing over at Temper, who is speaking with Saint. "It's really nice to see how you all treat each other."

"We get on each other's nerves, don't you worry," she adds, then lowers her voice. "Let me know how tomorrow goes with Temper."

I roll my eyes. "He's just taking me because you can't."

And apparently he doesn't want any of the other men taking me.

I don't even care if he's interested in me anymore

at this point. It feels like a week since we even had our epic date, but it was only yesterday, and so much has changed since then.

I've changed since then.

And so has he—in my eyes, anyway.

She smirks and says, "I didn't tell him I was busy working tomorrow. In fact, I'm doing nothing tomorrow."

My eyes widen. "Well then."

I guess *he's* still interested.

Chapter Nine

After a solid night's sleep, I wake up feeling much better than the day before. After a conversation with Ivy, which probably didn't give her any of the answers she wanted, I fell asleep in my new fluffy pajamas. With no alarm, I let my body determine how much rest it needed, and it seemed to have worked. I have a shower and dress in my new jeans and black off-the-shoulder long-sleeve top, loving the way they fit me.

Once I'm all ready to face the day, I unlock my bedroom door and step outside. The place is quiet, so everyone must have left, or those who don't live here have probably gone home.

"Temper?" I call out, heading for the kitchen.

I find him there, sitting in a white T-shirt and some shorts, a mug in his hands. "Good morning. How did you sleep?"

"Like a baby," I admit. "Being kidnapped is really tiring. Not that you'd know, since I'm guessing you're usually the kidnapper, not the kidnappee, but yeah, I was exhausted."

"Do you want some coffee?" he asks as he stands in front of the coffee machine, ignoring my comments, not taking the bait. "And something to eat? Or do you want to go out for breakfast?"

"Just coffee sounds great for now," I say, sitting down and watching him work his way around the kitchen. "Where is everyone?"

"At work," he says. "We run a few different businesses, and everyone always has somewhere they need to be. It's flexible, though, so if they have something else they need to do, someone will always cover for them."

"What kind of businesses?" I ask, being nosy.

"We have a bike shop, selling custom bikes," he explains and tells me all about the services they offer there. "We also have a bar, a club. We have our fingers in a few pies."

"I'll bet."

Illegal pies, no doubt.

My phone beeps with a message. Hey it's Izzy. I got Temper to send me your number. I've made you a list of the places you need to see and eat at before you leave. Enjoy your date!

I don't know about it being a date, but I know she's giving me shit from our conversation last night. "Izzy sent me a message."

"I gave your number to her, I didn't think you'd mind. You two seemed to have hit it off."

"No, I'm glad you gave it to her," I tell him. "Do you have any updates about the men who tried to shoot at you?"

"Not yet, but I'm working on it."

"What about information on the man who died, who he was, if anyone has any suspects, or if there was any camera surveillance?" I ask.

"There was no camera footage," he admits, sitting down next to me and sliding me my coffee. "And he hasn't been identified yet. No one seems to have any information on the man."

"Thank you," I say, blowing on the mug. "So you have nothing, and I'm stuck here until you do. My whole town must be in an uproar. I don't think we've ever had someone murdered there before."

"The police are keeping it quiet from what I've heard, probably for that reason. Did you decide where you want to go today? I thought we could take the bike, if you don't mind," he continues, watching me drink my coffee.

"That's fine," I tell him, remembering how much I enjoyed being on the bike with him. I show him Izzy's text message. "Can we go to one of these places? Maybe we should start at number one."

Temper laughs. "These are all food places."

"I know," I reply, shrugging and ducking my head. "We can eat and then you can take me somewhere. Maybe to one of your favorite places." I pause and then add, "Unless it's a strip club or something."

He chuckles under his breath. "I'm not that stupid. Let me have a quick shower and then I'll take you out for breakfast at one of the Isabella-approved places."

"Thank you," I call out as he leaves the room.

I keep myself busy by washing the few dishes in the sink and wiping down the counters while Temper gets ready. When he steps back into the room in jeans and a fresh black T-shirt, I can't help but check him out, even though I don't really want to. He's such a complex person, and I know he has many layers to him, but there's something about him that just draws me in. I look away, because I don't want him to catch me looking at him.

After everything that has happened, I shouldn't be looking at him like this. I've seen what these men are capable of, but it's not all black and white, and I'm finding that out firsthand. These men are the definition of shades of gray. Men you want on your side, not against you. They have no boundaries or limits.

They are good *and* bad.

I don't know where I want to stand with him—my emotions are all over the place. I want to lash out at him, but I also want him to keep me safe, and to take care of me.

The whole situation is fucked.

I don't want to forgive him for what he did to me, and I don't know if I ever completely will, but I can feel myself slowly giving in. He's obviously not all bad, kidnapping aside, and if I'm going to embrace my current predicament, maybe I should embrace him, too.

"You ready?" he asks, breaking me out of my thoughts.

"Yep. I want to grab my purse from the car, though," I say, walking past him with a little extra sway in my hips.

"I like the clothes you chose," he says from behind me, and I can practically feel his gaze.

"Probably good considering you paid for them all."

We stop at the car and I grab my handbag, slide my phone inside and cross the strap over me. "You ready for another adventure?" he asks, handing me a helmet.

"Always." I get on behind him, my arms tightly around his body, and the taste of freedom in my mouth.

"How old are you exactly?" I ask Temper as we sit in Eggslut eating delicious egg salad sandwiches. "When I first met you, I thought you were about midthirties."

"I was. Now I'm forty-two," he admits.

My eyes widen. "Okay, I didn't think you'd be that

old. You don't look that old." I don't know why forties sounds so much older than thirties.

His lip twitches. "I'll take that as a compliment. We have fourteen years between us. I thought you knew that."

"I don't know what I know," I grumble, making him laugh softly.

We do have a big age gap, which is quite intimidating. Obviously I knew he was older than me, but I didn't realize it was that substantial. I wonder if I come off as immature to him, especially as I remember giving him the finger yesterday, and all but stomping my feet and carrying on at him.

"The food is good," I state, changing the subject.

"It is," he agrees, taking a bite of his sandwich. "I haven't even been to most of the places on Izzy's list, so it's going to be a new experience for me, too."

"What, do you normally just stick to your usual places?" I ask.

"Yeah, there's a few places near the clubhouse that we go to a lot. Plus I'm usually too busy, and going out to eat at new places isn't high on the priority list," he explains.

"It should be. Food is one of the best things in the world," I say with a grin. "And you aren't too busy today."

"I'm taking time off. Can't let you leave here without having a proper L.A. experience, now can I?" He finishes the last bit of his meal.

"No, I guess not," I say, taking a sip of my juice. "What would your day normally consist of? MC stuff?"

Working in a bar that has lots of bikers passing through, I do hear enough to figure out how the whole MC thing works. People tend to see waitresses as invisible and talk freely in front of us. I don't know how Temper runs his club, but it will be interesting to see. They do treat each other like family, which is something different from what I've seen with other MCs.

"Taking care of anything that pops up, really. Problems with the businesses, or anything the men need me for. Making sure everything is running smoothly, and everyone is taken care of," he explains.

"So you're basically the dad of the entire MC," I conclude, leaning back in my seat and watching him. "Daddy Temper."

He laughs out loud. "Please don't call me that in public."

"What about when we aren't in public?" I can't help but ask.

His brown eyes darken and fill with heat. "Then it's fair play."

Clearing my throat, I look away, unable to take the intensity in his gaze. "Well, I'm ready to leave when you are."

"Where are we going?" he asks. "Home?"

"No," I reply, smirking. "Nice try, though. We're going to spend the rest of the day exploring the city." I want to see everything.

"I've had worse days," he teases, placing some money with a tip on the table.

"I'm paying for lunch," I announce, to which he laughs.

"No, you're not." But to his annoyance, I hand the waitress my credit card.

We leave Eggslut and head out on our next adventure, and throughout the rest of the day, I mentally tick off each place after each visit. I've never not worked, and this little kidnapping is starting to feel like a holiday.

As fucked-up as that sounds.

I worry about Mom, and if she's taking her medication and attending the appointments. I wonder if Ivy is cleaning the house, and if she knows how to do the inventory at Franks by herself. I've never even been away from my mom for more than a night or two, because she never allowed that. I even went to a local college so I could still live at home. I'm so out of my comfort zone right now, but it feels exhilarating.

Ivy messages me and I send her a picture back of me standing in front of the Hollywood sign. She now knows where I am for sure, and can put together that I'm not too far away at all. I feel bad that she's at home working and covering my shifts while I'm eating like a queen and sightseeing, but I promise to make it up to her when I get home. More than anything, I feel bad that she's the one who will have to listen to Mom worry and panic about where I am right now.

My mom has always had anxiety, and it has played a huge role in her parenting. I know it has a lot to do with her own childhood, and the lack of love she got from her parents. They didn't care what she did, they used to hit her anytime she did anything wrong, and she was always made to feel like she wasn't welcome in her own home. A childhood like that leaves its mark on a person, and I know she always wanted to be the mother she never had.

It's like she has tried to do the opposite with us, but in an unhealthy way. She's constantly worried about us, and has always been overly careful in everything we do. Helicopter parenting at its finest. She has always

instilled in us that there are things to fear, something I
had to teach myself to overcome as a teen. I don't think
I've realized how codependent and a little unhealthy
our relationship is until now. She's a good woman, and
I know she loves us more than anything, but she definitely has some issues she needs to work on.

When we get back to the clubhouse, Izzy has bought
a new suitcase for me and left it on my bed. I don't think
I've ever met such thoughtful people, especially from
people I haven't known long, and who aren't family. I
send her a quick message saying thank you, and asking her when she's free next so I can take her out for
lunch or something.

She replies instantly. How about tomorrow? Or is
Temper hogging you? I was thinking on Saturday night
Skylar and I could take you out and show you the night-
life?

I glance up as Temper sticks his head into my room.
"How come you get gifts? They never leave anything
for me on my bed. If they did it would probably be a
fuckin' prank."

"I'm going out with Skylar and Izzy on Saturday
night," I say, deciding to tell him not ask him. Why
should I have to ask him? He said I should enjoy my
time here, and I'm going to do just that.

"Okay," he replies, shrugging. "I'm going to cook
dinner, so I'll be in the kitchen." He cooks?

Daddy said yes, I text back, giggling to myself.

Izzy replies with a bunch of laughing emoji faces.

We only have the one small bar in my town, so that's
the extent of my experience, so I'm looking forward to
having a girls' night with them.

When I head to the kitchen, I find Temper in there

sitting up on the counter, reading something on his phone. "What are you doing?" I ask him.

"Reading a recipe for potato salad," he admits, placing the phone down. "I don't know if you can tell, but I'm not usually the one in the kitchen."

"Come on, I'll help you make everything," I say, hiding my smile. Side by side, we cook a roast with potato salad and peri peri corn for anyone who decides to drop in for dinner tonight.

I don't know what I pictured it would be like being with someone in an MC.

But it wasn't like this.

Chapter Ten

Saturday comes around and I'm wearing the red dress I bought with Izzy paired with some black strappy heels that Skylar lent me. With my hair down and my eyes rimmed in black kohl, I'm looking and feeling pretty damn good.

"So how are we getting there? A taxi?" I ask them as I put on my red lipstick in front of the mirror.

"Crow will take us," Skylar says, running her hands through her thick red hair. "He'll probably stay, too. There's no way the men are going to let us be there alone."

There's no anger or bitterness in her tone when she says that, so I can't help but ask, "Don't you guys mind that you can't go anywhere without someone watching you?"

"I can see why you would think that," Skylar admits, standing up from my bed and moving next to me at the mirror. "But when you've been through the shit we've been through, you can understand why it's a good idea to have one of the men around. Trouble doesn't just find us, it follows us around. And to keep us safe, it's in all of our best interest."

My eyebrows raise. "So what the hell am I supposed to expect tonight then?"

Skylar shrugs, her lip twitching. "Who knows? Just know we will all have each other's back and everything will be okay. You're going to have fun, so don't even stress. Just a few drinks, and a dance, and we'll take you to the hottest spots right now. I'm going to pour us some shots of Jäger to get this party started."

We leave my room and walk to the kitchen, then outside to have a drink before we head out. Skylar puts some music on, and it's not long before we're all chatting and laughing. Temper finds us, his eyes coming straight to me and taking me in from head to toe.

"Fuck," he grits out, and clears his throat. "You look beautiful, Abbie."

"Thank you," I reply, and I can feel my cheeks heating. He looks good himself, in a black collared shirt and jeans, and he smells even better. "What are you all dressed up for?"

"I'm coming with you," he says, grinning devilishly. "Didn't think I was going to miss out on the fun, did you?"

Skylar's eyes widen, and she pours herself another shot. "You've never voluntarily come out with us. Ever."

"That's not true," he denies, sitting down and pouring himself a drink. "What about in Vegas, Izzy? I went out with you then."

"Yeah, you did. But I'm pretty sure you sat there on your phone all night, nursing a glass of whiskey and avoiding anyone that tried to talk to you. I remember a few women tried to get your attention and you didn't as so much as give them a glance."

He ignores that comment. "I'll stay off my phone and will try to have a good time."

Skylar is still staring at him like she's only just met

him, a look of surprise etched on her face. "Who are you?"

When Saint and Renny also walk in, all dressed up to go out, we know exactly what's going on.

"What happened to a girls' night?" Skylar asks Saint, scowling. "We didn't invite you guys. We were expecting Crow to come, and that's it. Tonight is about Abbie having a good time, not you all marking your territory." The girls obviously like Crow, because they sound like they would have preferred that.

"We all want Abbie to have a good time too," Temper replies, sounding offended at the idea that they are coming for any other reason.

"That's why we're coming. We're the life of the party," Saint adds, grabbing Skylar around the waist and nuzzling her neck. "And Renny is going to drive, so I get to enjoy a drink with you."

Skylar turns to look at me, and I just shrug. I don't mind if they come.

Temper comes and sits down next to me, lifting his glass up to cheers with my shot glass. "To Abbie and her first night out with us."

"To Abbie!" everyone else chimes in, clinking glasses.

And that's how one very messy night begins.

"Oh my God, I love this song!" I say, not for the first time, pulling Temper to the middle of the dance floor and spinning around in a circle with my hands raised in the air. After drinking for over an hour at the clubhouse, Renny drove us to two clubs before we ended up here at club number three on drink number God knows what. I don't know how Renny has been putting up with us all night, with him being sober, but he's been patient as hell and laughing at all of our antics.

Temper's hands come around my waist as I grind my hips into a seductive circle, or at least I think that's what I'm doing. Temper's not much of a dancer, but he stands where he's meant to and moves with me, which I think is really cute. This is obviously not his ideal scene or weekend hangout, but he's putting in the effort to be here with me and I do appreciate that.

I've seen the way some of the women around us have been eying the men, and I guess it's hard not to; all three of them are appealing in their own way. I've never had to handle a situation like this before, and I can't help but feel a little jealous every time a beautiful woman looks in Temper's direction.

"Are you having a good time?" I ask, wrapping my arms around his neck and staring into his brown eyes.

"I am," he says in my ear. "Are you?"

I nod. "Are you kidding me? Tonight has been amazing. And the girls said trouble seems to follow them, but tonight has been drama free, so maybe I'm a good luck charm for you all."

Temper grins and dips me back, lips pressing against my jawline. "You're definitely my good luck charm. Does this mean that you forgive me for everything?"

I think about that. "I think I'll forgive you, but I'm not going to forget."

"So basically you're going to throw it in my face anytime I piss you off?"

"Most likely," I admit, closing my eyes and enjoying my happy buzz from the alcohol. "But come on, it wasn't something little. It was something a little big."

"A little big?" he teases, taking my hand and leading me back to the bar, where everyone else is.

"That's the first time I've seen you dance," Saint announces, sounding gobsmacked. "I don't even know what to say right now."

"I'd shut up if I were you," Renny mutters, elbowing Saint. "Let him have his fun."

"I'm just saying. Abbie, you bring out the fun in him. I haven't seen him smile so much in years," Saint says before ordering us another round of drinks.

I glance up at Temper with a big smile. "I like making you happy."

"I like smiling," he replies, wrapping his arm around me and tucking me under his side. "I don't know what it is about you, but from the second I saw you, I just wanted to be around you."

I kiss him then, going up on my tiptoes and cupping his stubbled cheek, making the first move for the first time in my life. Maybe it's the alcohol, maybe it's the beautiful words he's saying, or maybe it's me accepting my current fate, but there's no one else I'd rather be with right now.

"I'm glad I'm here," I say against his lips.

"Me too," he replies, pushing my hair back behind my ear.

Our eyes lock and hold for a few moments.

"Temper," Renny says to him, breaking up our moment.

Temper looks at him and Renny says something into his ear. Temper nods, his arm squeezing on my hip. "Let's get out of here," he says, a sense of urgency flashing in his eyes. "We can continue the party at home."

"Okay," I reply quickly, my attitude and demeanor changing with theirs. I look to Izzy and Skylar and they have worried expressions on their faces as they look at their men. Is something wrong? I scan the club but don't see anything or anyone out of place.

We leave, walking down the stairs, our group staying close together. Temper is first, holding my hand, with Renny and Izzy behind us and Skylar and Saint coming up the rear.

Crossing the road to get to the car is when shit hits the fan: four men appear out of the bushes, approaching us and pointing guns at Saint, Renny and Temper. The men quickly move in front of us, guarding all three of us women with their bodies.

"The girl comes with us," one of the men says, nodding toward me. "Otherwise, your women are going to be burying you."

Temper's eyes dart to me, and then back to the man making the demands. "Why do you want her?"

"She's the Knights of Fury MC president's woman. She has value," he says, smirking, his dark, beady eyes filled with smugness. "Yeah, we've been watching you. Hand her over, and the other women get to live."

"Why don't you tell me what you want from me now and save us the hassle?" Temper says in a calm tone, while he opens the car door and pushes me inside the driver's seat, in a quick, bold move that sets the shooters on edge.

"Don't move!" the man yells, hand now shaking, finger on the trigger. "I will kill you all."

What occurs next happens so fast that there isn't much time to panic. Temper and Saint charge at the men while Renny opens the car door, pushes Izzy and Skylar inside, and throws me the keys. I start the car, fingers trembling, and watch in horror while Temper fights two men, punching one in the face and taking his gun, which goes off, shooting into the air, while Saint and Renny take on the other two.

"We have to get out of here," Skylar says quickly from behind me, tone filled with panic. "The cops are going to come and we're all going to be fucked."

I don't know what comes over me next. I don't know if it's my flight-or-fight reflexes, or if it's because these men are specifically targeting me, but as soon as I get the opening, I throw the car into drive and press down on the gas. The car goes flying forward, knocking down the two men Temper was fighting, while he jumps out of the way.

Temper goes to help Saint and Renny when I yell, "Get in!" To them all.

All three manage to get into the car without anyone getting shot, half of the men on the ground from being run over and the other half injured from the beating they got.

"Drive!" Temper says from the front seat, and he doesn't need to tell me twice. I race out of there, keeping to the speed limit as to not draw any other extra attention to us, my fingers trembling on the wheel, my knuckles whiter than they've ever been.

"Holy fuck," I whisper to myself over and over again.

What have I done? I just literally ran over two men, and yes, they were trying to kidnap me at gunpoint, so they weren't necessarily upstanding citizens, but apparently neither am I.

"They were fine," Temper promises me, holding on to my knee and squeezing it. "They got back up as we drove off, okay? You didn't do any permanent damage."

"Okay." I nod, licking my dry lips. "I can't believe that just happened."

"I can't believe none of us got shot," Renny adds from the back seat.

"Or arrested," Saint adds.

Fuck.

When we're a safe distance away, I pull over on the side of the road. "Can you drive?" I ask Temper. I don't know the way back to the clubhouse, and with what just happened, I don't need the added stress of navigating a new city. Not to mention I've been drinking and am definitely over the limit. Although I feel extremely sober right now, I know that I'm not.

"I'll drive," Renny says, getting out of the car and swapping seats with me. He stops and gives me a big hug before I get in the back seat. "You okay?" he asks me softly.

I nod. "Yeah, I'll be fine."

Izzy wraps her arms around me as I get into the back seat. I have so many questions, but right now I'm in shock, and I just want to get home and pretend this whole thing never happened.

I seem to be doing that a lot since inviting Temper into my life.

I guess the girls were right—trouble really does follow them around.

Chapter Eleven

"They must have followed us, and saw you and Abbie kissing in the club," Renny says to Temper, pacing back and forth in the living room. "And thought they'd take her in revenge for what happened."

Renny eyes Izzy, who looks confused, and I only just remember that she still doesn't know about him killing that guy.

"Revenge for what?" she asks, frowning. "What am I missing here? Didn't they shoot at you guys last time? Shouldn't it be us wanting revenge, not them?"

"They did come out of fuckin' nowhere shooting at us," Renny agrees, grimacing. "But I also shot back at them, and one of them was…injured."

"How injured?" Izzy presses, brow furrowing.

"We think he's dead," Temper admits, rubbing the back of his neck. "And that's why I brought Abbie back, because she saw the whole thing."

Izzy's jaw drops open. "Why didn't you tell me this, Renny? What the fuck? And you brought Abbie back because she was a witness to this whole thing and you didn't want her to talk?"

"Temper brought Abbie back," Renny corrects, brown eyes filled with concern. "It was a messed-up situation, but they came at us, and I did what I had to do to protect us."

Izzy softens, her shoulders dropping. "Why didn't you just tell me the truth, though? You had to have known this was going to come out eventually."

"I didn't want you to look at me different. I killed someone, okay? It's not exactly something I'm proud of. I see his face every time I close my eyes, so I'm not exactly handling it well," he admits, looking down at his hands.

Izzy moves closer and hugs him. "I'm not going to look at you any different. I know the man you are. I do want you to be honest with me, though. I don't want to have to find out things like this after they happen. That's what I'm hurt about."

The two of them leave to talk things through, while the rest of us try to come up with a game plan.

"We need to find everything we can on them," Temper announces, looking to Saint. "Who they are, what they want. What their problem with us is. Before we couldn't remember any of the faces of the men who shot at us, but this time we got a good look at them. We can find out who they are."

"I'm already on it," Saint responds from the couch, arm around Skylar. "I'm going to get the surveillance footage of what happened."

"How?" I can't help but ask.

He leans forward to look at me, grinning. "I have my ways. Let's just say the club owner owes me a favor or two."

"So what happens when you find out who they are?" I ask with eyes wide. This whole world is new to me. I have no idea what is normal and what is not.

"Let's see what we're dealing with first," Temper

says, offering me his hand. "Come on, let's get to bed. It's three in the morning."

I don't know if I'm going to be able to sleep after everything, but I can try. Temper grabs us both a bottle of water and walks me to my room.

"Can I get you anything? Painkillers?" he asks, watching me open the water and drink half of it in one gulp.

"I have some in my handbag; I'll be okay," I reply, and then pause, and ask him, "Would you mind lying down with me until I fall asleep?"

I feel like a little baby asking, but I just want him near me right now. Tonight has been full of mixed emotions between us, and then with everything that happened afterward. It's been a lot, and I know I'm going to be up all night replaying everything and overthinking if he's not with me.

"Of course," he says, stepping inside my room and turning the light on. "I'll have a quick shower and be back, okay?"

I nod, and take the time to do the same, having a shower and removing my makeup before getting dressed in my pajamas.

He's lying in my bed when I come out, shirtless, in nothing but a pair of silk boxers. It's the first time I'm seeing his bare chest, and I'm actually taken aback at how muscular he is, his six-pack defined and flawless, and his large biceps proof of his strength.

"Are you sure you don't go to the gym?" I ask, swallowing hard. "Because you really look like you go to the gym." I'm suddenly feeling a little frumpy, my body having no definition whatsoever.

"No, I don't." He chuckles. "I box here with the men, run, and I do a lot of physical work. I live a fit and healthy lifestyle."

"I can see that," I say, sliding into the bed and under the covers. We lie facing each other. "I probably should have turned off the light."

He smiles widely, and it hits me right in the chest. "I'll get it."

He turns the light off and joins me back in bed. Just like I thought, it's comforting being next to him, and when his arms come around me I can't help but feel safe and protected.

"I'm sorry for all the shit I've dragged you into," he whispers, kissing my temple. "I never should have asked you out on that date."

My life would have been much easier if he hadn't, but for some reason I can't seem to regret ever getting to know him. "It's not like you planned for all of this to happen," I reply, yawning.

And my actions today proved how easy it is to make certain decisions to protect yourself and your friends. I never thought I'd be capable of doing what I did, purposely running someone over with a car.

How the mighty have fallen.

Still, against Temper, I sleep like a baby.

I wake up alone, and to my phone ringing. "Hello?" I say.

"Hey, how are you?" Ivy asks. "Mom wants to speak to you."

Shit. I'd been speaking to Mom through Ivy, but I knew I could only get away with that for so long.

"Abbie?"

"Hey, Mom," I say, rubbing my eyes and sitting up. "Is everything okay?"

"My daughter left without saying a word; do you think everything is okay? When are you coming home? Ivy said you'd just be gone for a few days and you're in Los Angeles of all places," she rattles off. "I don't know what you're thinking, Abbie. You know how much I need you here. I forgot my medication yesterday because you weren't here to remind me, and I've had to up the dose of my anxiety medication because I've been so stressed."

I consider how to answer her. "I'm sorry I left without saying anything. It was a last-minute decision, and I'll be back soon," I say. "And you're a grown woman; I'm sure you can remember to take your pills. Just set an alarm on your phone, or ask Ivy to remind you."

She pauses and then says, "I'm worried about you. This doesn't seem like you at all, Abbie. This just isn't in your character. I've waited three days, but now I want you to come home. Enough is enough, and we need you here. Poor Ivy has enough on her plate. She has to manage college and cover your shifts at Franks."

Guilt fills me, but it's not like I can just return, especially after what happened last night. Ivy can manage just fine; Mom is the one struggling. "I will make it up to Ivy," I promise. "But I can't come just yet, Mom. I'll be home soon, though, okay? So don't worry. I'm fine. Did Ivy show you the pictures of me?"

"Yes, I saw them," she says, sighing. "I just don't understand why you went on a random holiday without saying anything to us. What aren't you telling me?"

A lot.

"Nothing, Mom," I lie. "I have to go, but I'll call you soon, okay?"

"Abbie—"

"I love you both, bye," I say, quickly hanging up before she can guilt trip me any further.

"Fuck," I whisper to myself, groaning and rolling over, and hide my phone under my pillow, like that's going to save me. How long am I going to be able to get away with this? She's not going to accept this from me for very long, and the last thing I want to do is stress her out when her health is only just improving.

Forcing myself out of bed, I get ready for the day then head to the kitchen for some coffee. I smile when there's a note on the table with some calla lilies lying on top it. Picking them up, I admire them before reading the note.

Had to leave early to sort some things. I'll be home around twelve to take you out for lunch. Crow is here to get you anything you need. P.S. Last night was the best sleep I've had in years.

Smiling, I hold the note to my chest, just as Crow steps in and goes, "Isn't that fuckin' cute?" making me jump and scaring the shit out of me.

"Jesus Christ, Crow," I say, spinning around to face him.

He simply grins, leaning against the doorframe. His jeans are extra tight today, the denim the same color as his eyes. "Who knew the prez had a romantic side."

"I don't know why you all give him so much shit; he's a nice guy," I say, defending him. I mean, at least he is to me.

"He is a good man. Around you he shows a different side, though, one we aren't used to, which is why we're all in shock," Crow replies, running a hand through his blond hair. "Now I've been told I need to make sure you have something for breakfast. Do you want to eat out or in?"

"Out," I say, placing the note back down on the table. I want to do something nice for Temper, and I have a plan.

Chapter Twelve

"How are you feeling after what happened last night?" Crow asks as we head to the grocery store. "Imagine if it was just me with you three ladies? I would have been fucked. And if anything happened to any of you, Temper, Saint and Renny would have killed me three times over."

"Babysitting gig comes with a lot of pressure, doesn't it?"

He laughs. "It's more than that. The men trust me to look after the women they love, and that's no small feat. I could be doing much worse as a prospect, trust me."

"They must trust you a lot," I say, staring at his profile. "You're really easy to get along with, so no one even minds if you're tagging along either."

"Well, that's nice of you to say. I guess if you compare anyone to Chains they'd be nice, though," he jokes, parking the car.

"Yeah, you two are kind of opposites," I admit. Crow is light, Chains is dark, in temperament and appearance.

"He's not a bad guy," Crow adds, opening his door and glancing back at me. "Let's do this."

We head inside and I grab all the things needed for

an impromptu picnic, complete with wine, platter foods and various cheeses.

"This is something a man would like, right?" I ask as we put the bags in the truck and get back in the car. "I mean, if someone planned a little picnic for you and put in some effort to show you that they appreciate you, you'd enjoy it?"

"Are you kidding me? He's going to love it," he assures me. "And it's the perfect day for it. The sun's out, and he's probably going to be stressed as fuck from trying to do damage control from last night."

"I'm sure you can tell I'm a little out of my element." I groan.

I have no experience with men. And the first man I actually like had to be complicated as fuck, in a motorcycle club, and come with a whole lot of baggage.

"You'll be fine. He seriously likes you, Abbie. Everyone does. And you know what, that's important, because if you and he get together you're going to be someone that people look up to. Being the president's old lady isn't a role for everyone."

"Okay, I wasn't thinking that far ahead, but thanks for adding that on," I mumble, my mind pushing back that comment for another day's problem.

Crow just shrugs. He meant it, this is actually a thing, and if anything progresses with me and Temper, it's something I'm going to have to think about. However, with me having to go home at the quickest opportunity, I think that this is where everything is going to end. That doesn't mean I won't enjoy the time with him that I have, because I'm going to make the most of every second.

We grab some bagels for breakfast and then head

back to the clubhouse. I tidy the place up, wanting to do something productive with my time, while Crow works out in their gym. When it gets close to lunch-time, I create a platter and set up a little picnic blanket outside, making it as cute as possible, pillows ready for us to sit on. With a bottle of wine in a tub of ice, I work with what I have, and am pretty happy with how it turned out.

"It looks good enough to be on a social media post," Crow says, walking out shirtless from his workout, a light sheen of sweat glistening in the sunlight.

"Thanks," I say, shrugging, suddenly feeling a little unsure of myself. Temper is the president of an MC—is something like this going to be stupid and trivial to him? Maybe he's busy and won't even be able to return when he said he would, and then Crow is going to have to eat this platter with me so I don't look like a dickhead.

"Hey," Temper says from behind us, and we both spin around.

"Hey," I reply, watching Crow make a quick exit.

"What's all this?" Temper asks, smiling as he takes in the little setup. "Is this for me?"

I nod, shifting on my feet, feeling awkward as hell. "Yeah, I thought I'd do something…nice…" I trail off, apparently unable to speak coherently. Clearing my throat, I sit down and pat the spot next to me. "Would you like some wine?"

"I'd love some," he says, sitting down and eyeing the selection in front of him. "This looks amazing, Abbie. You're so fuckin' cute, you know that?"

I breathe a sigh of relief, and pour us both some wine. "I just thought you might want to chill out and relax a little after…everything."

"I could say the same for you," he says quietly, taking the glass from my hand, our fingers touching. "This must be a lot for you, and you've been handling it so well. We're used to shit like this going down; you're not."

"Yeah, true, but it's up to you to fix it all, not me, which means the pressure is all on you."

"True," he agrees, lifting his glass. "Cheers."

"Cheers." I cut some brie and place it on a cracker. "How did this morning go?"

"Saint is viewing the surveillance as we speak and then destroying it so we can't get into any shit," he explains, brown eyes watching me as I eat. "But then we need to try to identify these guys. We're going to have to pull in some favors, which I hate doing, but it's kind of necessary. Anyway, let's just enjoy this moment and not think about what's to come."

"Sounds good. Thank you for the flowers and the note you left this morning," I say, smiling at him. "They were beautiful."

"If you want to see beautiful, you should have seen how you look when you're asleep," he blurts out, gaze going to the wineglass. "I struggled to leave you this morning. You know, I'm not usually a cuddler, I prefer to have my space in bed, but I liked having you next to me. It's peaceful. Somehow you drown out all the stress and worry."

I can't wipe the smile off my face. "I don't even know what to say to that. I like that I'm different for you."

"You have no idea." He smiles. "I spoke to my brother yesterday, and he's in shock. I think he thought I'd be a bachelor for the rest of my life."

"Are you two close?" I ask.

He nods. "Yep, he's all the blood family I have. Trade and those kids of his, I'd do anything for them. What about you? Are you close with your family? I know that you're close with Ivy."

"I am." I grin, thinking about her. "I'm close with my mom too, but we have a more complicated relationship. With her it's almost like the roles have reversed, and she needs me to look after her, which makes it pretty stressful. She's made me feel really guilty being away from home, making it sound like she can't cope without me, and that her anxiety is in full throttle."

"Oh, that sucks. I'm sorry that I put you in this position, but that's not very fair," he says, frowning. "A child should never have to sacrifice for a parent. You should be living your life how you want to. Life is short, you know? And your mom is an adult. I'm sure she can learn to be self-sufficient without you."

"That's what I'm hoping for."

We nibble at the food, drink wine in the sunshine and just enjoy each other, pretending that we're a normal couple on a date, and it's wonderful.

If only things were this easy. If only he were a local guy I met, a banker or something, and we could have this every day.

But he's not, and I knew that coming into this, so I can't place all the blame on him.

And when Saint comes into the garden and tells Temper he needs to speak to him, I know that we're back to reality.

"You go. I'll tidy up," I tell him, feeling a little giddy from either the wine or the company.

"Are you sure?" he asks, leaning forward and giving me a quick yet gentle kiss. "No one has ever done something like this for me before, so thank you. It's not something I'm going to forget."

Another kiss, this time on my forehead, and then he follows Saint back inside. Wishing there was more wine, I pack everything up and head back inside. The men are nowhere to be found, so I lie back down on my bed and send a message to Izzy.

Abbie: What are you and Skylar up to today?

She responds by adding Skylar to a group chat, and then typing:

Izzy: Skylar is at work, but I'm at home. Do you want me to come over? I should take my dog for a walk anyway.

Abbie: Yes, please. Something is going down and the men are in a meeting.

Izzy: Be there in twenty.

I'm sitting on the couch watching a movie when Skylar comes in, her gorgeous staffy mix by her side. "This is Shadow," she says, patting his head.

"Hello, cutie," I say to him, and laugh when he jumps on the couch and starts licking my face. "He's adorable."

"He is." She sits down next to me. "They still haven't come out?"

"Nope. I don't know what's going on," I admit, pausing the movie and giving Izzy my full attention. "I ran over two men last night."

She waves her hand in the air. "They were fine. They got back up."

"Still," I reply, pursing my lips. "Would you have done the same if you were in my situation?"

"Hell yes I would have," she says instantly, brow furrowing. "You did what any of us would have done, Abbie. You're not a bad person. It wasn't you with a gun, making threats. We were just trying to get us all out of there safely. So don't you feel guilty, not even for one second."

I nod. It's good to hear those words from her. "Okay, you're right. I did what I had to."

"You did," she assures me. "Who knows what would have happened if you didn't do that? It was four against three and they all had guns. It's a miracle we all got out of there unscathed."

"I've never even seen a gun in real life before all of this," I admit, blinking slowly. "Now I feel like I should probably know how to use one."

"You should. Ask Temper, he's a pro."

"I bet he is." I groan, scrubbing my palm down my face. I'm updating her on the little picnic I did for him when he walks into the room.

"We found out who the men are," he says to us both, just as Saint steps into the room. "Mercenaries. They are former soldiers. The best you can get around our parts. Someone has hired them, and paid them very well, to follow us, get information and kill me, or kill some of us, or basically just fuck shit up with the MC."

"Who would want to do that?" I ask, glancing between the two men. "Just how long is your list of enemies?"

No one answers me.

Great.

"All the men are coming in now and we're going to

discuss it and come up with a plan," Temper says, patting Shadow when he comes up to him. "We're going to need all of you to stay safe—don't go anywhere alone, and keep tabs on each other, all right? We're back on high alert until we take care of these men."

We all nod.

He looks to Saint. "Where's Skylar?"

Saint puts his phone in his pocket. "I just texted and asked her to come home. She was working, but she'll be here soon."

What a mess.

It's safe to say my problems of being stuck in my hometown seem less complicated than ever. These new problems of life and death are making me realize how much I took my life for granted. At the same time, though, being out and away, and having this freedom also makes me realize how much I've been missing, and how I haven't really been living life. I've just been following the rules and existing the way my mother wants me to.

"Want to go for a ride?" Temper asks, offering me his hand.

"Sure," I reply, taking it.

And then there are moments like this, when it's just me and him, that are perfect.

And worth it.

Chapter Thirteen

I didn't really get to speak with Trade on the first night that I met him, because all the members of the MC were there, but tonight it's just him and his kids having dinner with us, giving a more personal and intimate setting.

His son, AJ, is such a bright kid, and with his dark hair tied up in a man bun just like his dad's, and his long lashes and cute dimpled smile, he is definitely going to be a heartbreaker.

"This is so yummy, Uncle Tommy," he says to Temper, beaming. Trade's kids are the only ones I've ever heard calling Temper by his real name, and it's a little weird to hear, but also super cute.

"Is it? I made it myself," Temper says to his nephew, grinning.

AJ eyes the chocolate cake. "No you didn't. I bet you bought it at the store. I've never seen you bake a day in your life."

"He made me a cake once," Alia adds, licking the chocolate from her fingers. "Well, at least he tried to make me a cake."

"Hey, that was an artistic creation," Temper says to his niece, pretending to be offended. "It came straight from a packet and I had to follow the extremely complicated instructions."

"You just had to add eggs and water and mix it all together," she says, looking at her dad. "The two of you have the same skills in the kitchen."

"What do you guys eat every night?" I ask her, trying to hide my smile and failing hard.

"Easy stuff, like meat and salad," she says, pouting her lips out, and resting her face on her hand. "Or Ariel will cook us something really nice and yummy, like a homemade lasagna or seafood pasta."

"That does sound yummy." I know Ariel is Izzy's sister, and her and Trade seem super cute together.

"Ariel is a really good cook," India adds. She's the oldest, and the quietest of the lot, but is such a gorgeous, well-mannered child. Trade has done so well raising these three. I don't know where their mother is, but no one has mentioned it, and I'm sure as hell not going to ask.

"So, I've heard a lot about you, Abbie," Trade says when he finds me in the kitchen alone. "But nothing directly from you."

"Well, I was in school, but I've put that on hold for now while I help my family with our business. I will definitely finish my degree, because that's something I've always wanted for myself," I say, rinsing my dish and placing it in the dishwasher. I turn to face him with a tea towel in my hands, wiping them.

"Do you like kids?" he asks, studying me, as if by looking into my eyes he can see if I'm a good person or not.

"I do. Do you?" I fire back.

His lip twitches. "Yes. Do you think you could handle the whole MC thing? I mean, I left the MC for my kids, because as you've found out, it's not always the safest environment."

"I didn't know that you weren't in the MC," I admit, putting the towel down and pulling out a chair at the table to sit. "I didn't realize that just walking away was a thing."

"It's not," he agrees, cringing as he also takes a seat. "It's something that follows you around forever, and once you're allied with the MC, you always are."

So does he just tell himself he's not a member just to make himself feel better about the situation? Or is he hoping that the MC drama won't always touch him? With his closest family member as the Knights president, I don't think he can ever walk away unscathed, because anything that happens to Temper, and therefore the club, will always affect him.

"And you didn't answer my question," he presses.

"I don't know," I reply in all honesty. "I've kind of being thrown into this situation, and I have no idea what's going to happen. I do like Temper. I like being around him. I like how he makes me feel, like I'm invincible, and I want nothing but for him to be happy."

"But?"

"But I do need to go home. I have responsibilities there, and I want to go back to college and I don't know how many more kidnappings I'm going to be able to handle."

Trade surprises me by laughing. "You guys will figure it all out. It always has a way."

"What always has a way?" I ask, resting my elbows on the table.

"Love."

My mouth opens and closes. "Ummmm…"

He laughs some more, just as Temper comes in, just in time to save me from this conversation. He's so good with the kids, and it's just so nice to watch them all interacting together.

I'm not going to lie, it's sexy as hell.

Love, though?

I don't know about that one.

Staring down at my mom's name on my phone, I wince and reject the call. I just don't know what to say to her, and I know she's going to kill me for not returning home already. I wish I could explain the situation to her properly, but I can't, and I know she's worried, but the less she knows, the better. It's just such a shitty situation, but I wish she would stop treating me like a child, because at the end of the day I'm an adult and I've told her that I'm okay and will be returning home when I can.

I never realized how bad our relationship was until I got here. Seeing how she's behaving—demanding I come home, scolding me for leaving, calling me at least five times a day—is making me realize that I've been living my life according to her. What she wants, what she needs. She's never really encouraged me to do anything for me. It's always been about her.

"You going to answer that?" Temper asks, cuddling up to me. When he asked me if I wanted him to sleep with me again, I said yes. I like being next to him.

"Nope. She's going to ask for answers I can't give her right now. I'll send her a voice message or something so she knows I'm fine," I explain, rolling over to face him. "I wouldn't be surprised if she comes out here to find me. I really need to give her a date that I'm returning or something."

"Tell her in a week," he says, tucking my hair back behind my ear. "I'll take you back myself. If shit's not sorted, I'll stay with you until it is and make sure that you're safe, all right?"

"That's a bit cute," I whisper, smiling. "Okay, I'll tell her one week."

"You're going to be missed around here when you leave," he says, brown eyes scanning mine. He leans forward and presses a kiss against my lips. My eyes squeezed shut, I melt into the kiss, moving closer to him, deepening the kiss. His fingers run along my hair, gently bunching a handful in his fist, pulling my head back for easier access to my lips. He's such a good kisser, I could never tire of his lips.

When he pulls away, I whisper, "Don't stop."

And then his lips are back on mine, and then they're traveling down my jawline, my neck, my collarbone. Sitting up, I remove my pajama top, my breasts free, and then I tug at his tank, wanting him to remove it too. Once it's off, I press my breasts against his chest, the skin-on-skin contact sending shivers down my spine.

Taking control, Temper pushes me to my back and worships my body, kissing me everywhere, stroking me with his fingers, until he slides his hand under my pants and against my pussy. I'm not wearing any underwear, my skin soft and just shaven, and he continues to stroke the sensitive skin, eventually sliding his finger inside of me, the wetness coating him.

"So tight," he murmurs, kissing me deeper. I've only been with one man, once, but I do have a vibrator that has been my stand-in, so it's not like nothing has ever been down there.

Working his way down my body, he pulls my pants down with his teeth, and I lift my hips to help him.

"Are you on the pill?" he asks, and I nod.

"Good," he whispers, placing his face right in front of my pussy. He breathes in deeply and groans, as if he loves the scent of me, then peeps his tongue out for a little taste, which seems to send him over the edge, because the next minute he's eating me out like he's starving, licking and sucking, rubbing his tongue against my clit and sending me into overdrive.

I thought men don't know where the clit is? briefly runs through my mind, before pleasure, desire and want consume my every thought and feeling. When I come, it's powerful, strong, and seems to go on forever.

"Fuck," I whisper, my legs trembling, my back arched and my mouth open of its own accord.

Before I can even come back to myself, Temper is taking his shorts off, setting himself free. He looks to me as if for permission, and when I nod and slide against him, he slowly works himself inside of me. His penis is huge, much bigger than the only other one I've seen, but it feels so good, and I'm so wet, dampness all over my thighs.

Leaning down, he kisses my lips. "Are you okay?"

I nod. "More than okay."

"You feel so fuckin' good, I almost just came sliding inside of you," he admits, groaning.

"You're really good at all of this stuff," I whisper, and moan as he bends his head to suck on my nipple.

"I'm glad you think so." Things get hot and heavy, but before he can come, he pulls out and lies back. "Sit on my face, I want to taste you again."

Holy fuck.

Chapter Fourteen

I wake up smiling before my eyes are even open.

"Good morning, beautiful," he says from next to me. "I made you some coffee."

I don't think today could get any better.

"Thank you," I say, my voice thick with sleep. Pushing my hair out of my face, I rub my eyes before accepting the mug of deliciousness.

"How did you sleep?" he asks.

I flash him a sideways glance. "Pretty damn well, and yourself?"

He grins in response. "I don't know about you, but it's been a fuckin' long time for me, so I'm feeling damn good."

We never had the chat about how many people we'd slept with, or when, but apparently we're going to have it now.

"It's been a long time for me too," I admit, suddenly looking down into my coffee. "I've umm…only actually slept with one person. One time."

And it was shit.

Last night showed me just how amazing sex can be, especially if it's with the right person. Temper gave me my first orgasm that wasn't self-induced, and let me tell you, it was a fucking out-of-body experience. I don't know how I'm supposed to go back to my vibrator after that. The connection, the sensations, the touching... it was honestly a night that I'm never going to forget.

"Really?" he asks, eyes going wide. "How? Look at you—you must get hit on all the time working at the bar."

"I kind of just stick to myself. I mean, I have been asked out before, but never by anyone I was interested in. I don't know, I guess I was just waiting for the right man to come along," I explain, looking back at him. "I feel comfortable with you, but have butterflies at the same time. I don't know. You make me feel confident and beautiful just by the way you look at me. I thought I'd have felt a little shy last night, being naked in front of you, but I didn't."

"Good," he says, smiling at me. "I want you to feel that way, always. I don't think you know how amazing you are, Abbie."

I reach out and take his hand. We're getting closer every day and showing him affection is becoming more and more natural. I don't know how we got here, but here we are. I'm trying not to overthink it, and I'm just going to go with the flow.

Chains is sitting shirtless in the kitchen with the newspaper and his coffee by the time I make it in there. I haven't really seen anyone under fifty reading the newspaper because everyone has news apps on their phone these days.

He doesn't even lift his head when I walk past him and put some bread in the toaster, and I think he's going to ignore me completely until he says, "There's some bacon and eggs in the pan if you want some. I even mashed some avocado."

"Thanks," I say, eying the pan, and serve some on my plate. "It looks good."

"I used to be a chef," he admits, giving me the first bit of personal information he's ever given me. "Before I became a prospect."

Surprised by his admission, I stop in my tracks and turn to face him. "Really? Do you cook much here for everyone?"

"Nope" is all he gives me.

"Okay," I reply, dragging the word out. I'm not sure if he's just not a people person, or if he just gives no shits about how he comes across, but he's definitely the most unfriendly of the men here.

"Just the woman I was looking for," Dee says, clapping his hands together when he spots me. "I need to go shopping, and I need someone without a penis to come with me."

"I'm taking her to the shooting range today," Temper says as he joins us, slapping him on the back. "What the fuck you need to go shopping for, huh?"

"Clothes," Dee replies, glancing down at his worn T-shirt. "I need to buy some new clothes, and I have no fashion sense."

"We're on a fuckin' lockdown, and you're worried about clothes?" Temper deadpans, turning to me and shaking his head. "Want to learn how to shoot today?"

I nod. "Yeah, actually that sounds good." Seems like it's something important to learn while I'm here, maybe with some kind of self-defense moves and perhaps even whatever driving course police are made to do, for the next time I'm stuck driving the getaway vehicle.

"Good," he says, smiling at me and disappearing again.

"Him smiling so much is fuckin' weird," Dee comments, watching the space where Temper just was. "I don't know how I'm going to get used to it."

Moving to the table with my full plate, I pull out a chair and dig in. "He has a great smile."

Chains lifts his head and looks at me, his dark eyes giving nothing away. "He's much happier with you around, that's for sure."

"Thank you," I say. "And thank you for this delicious breakfast."

"You're welcome," he replies, turning his attention back to his newspaper.

Once I'm ready, I go find Temper, who is in the gym boxing with Saint. I know he says he doesn't work out, but this looks like a workout to me, the two of them punching each other, swerving and ducking. They're both shirtless, in nothing but shorts, and I can't look away from Temper, flashbacks from last night hitting me. Him on top of me, him behind me, him going down on me.

My face heating, I leave the gym only to run into Skylar, almost knocking her phone out of her hands. "Shit, sorry," I say, grabbing her arms.

"Sorry, I should be paying attention to where I'm going instead of on my phone," she says, hands on her chest but a smile on her face. "Is Saint in there?"

I nod. "Yeah, him and Temper are boxing."

"Quite the sight, isn't it?" she asks, smirking. "Do you want to come and sit with me outside until they're done?"

"Sure," I say, following her out and sitting down on one of the comfy outdoor seats. "You're off today?"

"Yeah, I've taken a few days off until this whole thing calms down," she explains, putting her phone on the table. "I'm a paramedic, and I won't be able to concentrate at work if I'm wondering what the hell is going on back here, you know? I'd rather be here, making sure everyone is okay. I hate when shit like this is going down. I was supposed to go to my brother's house tonight, but I'm just going to stay here and chill."

"It's definitely stressful," I agree, looking out over the yard. "How often does things like this happen?"

"You just never know." She sighs, twirling her red hair around her finger. "It's been at least eight months since the Izzy drama happened. It's so easy to get lulled into a false sense of safety, and then before you know it some other bullshit happen and you're back on alert again. I'm not going to lie, it's not always easy being who we are."

"I can see that," I say softly.

It's just, how do you walk away from these men?

How am I going to walk away from Temper?

"Why is nothing easy?" I ask, pursing my lips. "I finally found a man that I like, and who likes me, and it has to come with so many complications and sacrifices."

"Nothing worth anything is easy," she says, flashing me a sympathetic look. "I've known Temper for as long as I can remember, ever since I was a kid."

"Really?" I ask, eyebrows rising.

"Yeah, my mom used to date the old president, Hammer, so I spent some of my childhood here, with the men," she explains, smiling sadly. "So I've loved Temper for a long time. He's family to me, and I can honestly say that you've made such a change in him. He's happier, and lighter. He smiles, he laughs. I haven't even heard him raising his voice. He's a new man."

"You know, Temper's been asking me out since I met him five years ago, and back then I felt like he was too old for me. But now that I think about it, I don't think I ever thought he was too old for me—I thought I was too young for him. Like I was too immature."

Skylar starts laughing. "How old are you?"

"Twenty-eight."

"So he's like…what, fourteen years older than you? Age is nothing but a number."

"A number that haunts us women the older we get," I grumble.

"At least you'll always be young compared to him," she teases, laughing at her own joke.

"That's true." And I'm not going to complain about the experience he has, in the bedroom and out of it.

We end up chatting for ages, and when Temper and Saint emerge—Temper showered and dressed in all black, ready to teach me how to shoot—we're both laughing in hysterics and they look at us like we're crazy.

"You ready for this?" he asks me.

"I'm ready."

"Let's make you badass."

Chapter Fifteen

"I'm enjoying this a little more than I probably should," I admit, aiming at the target. "This is actually pretty fun."

And kind of like a stress release. It also makes me feel a little less helpless. Like before this, if someone had thrown me a gun and told me to defend myself, I would have no idea what to do with it. I mean, yeah, point it and pull the trigger, but there's a little more to it than that, and it's good to know how to use this weapon safely. I don't think I'm going to be taking this up as a hobby or anything, but it feels good to have this knowledge under my belt. It's been a great experience, and having Temper standing behind me with his arms over me, showing me the ropes, has also been quite enjoyable.

It also helps that I'm a good shot.

I shoot, and it hits the target right in the middle.

"Remind me not to make you angry," Temper comments from my side, but I can hear the pride in his tone.

"Yeah, you better not. Seriously, though, I do feel better now knowing how to use one of these things," I admit, safely putting the gun away. "Do you come here often?"

"Not really anymore," he says, pulling me into his arms. "Trade and I used to come here a lot. After becoming president, it's like I just haven't got the time to do the things I enjoy. Since you've been here this is the most time I've taken off… I think ever. I'm usually in meetings, running around and making sure all the businesses are being taken care of, making sure the men aren't getting into too much shit."

"And who makes sure you aren't getting into too much trouble?" I ask, resting my cheek against his chest. "And that you're being taken care of?"

He runs his fingers through my hair. "I take care of myself."

I glance up at him. "Skylar says you're happier now than you've been in a long time."

"I can agree with that," he says, leading me back to the car. "Kind of hard not to be, isn't it?"

I don't know how he can be so damn cute. I sent my mom a voice mail on the way to the shooting range telling her I will be home in a week, and that she doesn't need to worry about me, everything is fine.

If I'm being honest, though?

I hope this week goes slow as hell.

"We have a fuckin' problem," Renny says as he steps into the clubhouse. Saint, Temper and I are sitting out the back with music on and a drink in our hands. Skylar just left with Chains to grab groceries.

"What is it?" Temper asks, sitting forward.

"I ran into one of our clients at the bike shop, and he mentioned that Grayson Palmer has been asking around about us. Does that name sound familiar to you?" he asks his president.

"Palmer...the drug dealer?" Temper asks, sharing a look with Saint. "What does that fucker want with us? We don't deal with drugs."

"Anymore, anyway," Saint mumbles.

"He's not just a dealer anymore, he's moved up to the fuckin' kingpin," Renny continues, pulling out a chair and sitting down, knees spread wide, elbows on his thighs. "He runs one of the biggest drug cartels in Southern California. And I don't know what he wants with us, but we need to find out immediately. It's enough we have mercenaries after us—last thing we need is some drug lord adding to our current list of enemies."

"Palmer can get in line at this point," I grumble.

"We've had no dealings with him, no bad blood," Temper thinks out loud, strumming his fingers on the table. "There are two options here: either this is just a coincidence that he's been asking about us and there are mercenaries after us, or the more obvious conclusion is that he works with the mercenaries. Or, fuck, even hired them. How do we know they aren't his henchmen?"

"We don't." Saint nods, standing up and grabbing his phone off the table. "What if we just go and speak to him?"

"Palmer?" Renny asks, looking to Temper. "What do you think we should do?"

"Let's find out more about this Palmer guy before I decide," Temper says. "I need to know exactly what we're working with here. I don't want to go in blind. Saint, call the rest of the men in."

"On it," Saint says, sending out a text message.

Drug lords, mercenaries...what other kinds of people am I going to meet during the next few days? I stay quiet during their conversation, and when Renny and Saint leave to figure out what move to make next, Temper and I are left alone again.

"I'm going to go to Izzy's house with a pitcher of margaritas," I tell Temper. I know we're supposed to be on a lockdown, but I seriously can't think of anything better right now, because this whole thing is just too much, and she only lives down the road.

I make up some margaritas and am about to leave as Crow and Dee walk up. "Where were you guys?" I ask them, eying Dee's unbuttoned shirt. "I'm guessing you didn't find anyone with taste to go shopping with you, then?"

"We were at the strip club, working," he admits, glancing down at his shirt. "And no, apparently none of my female friends can make time for me." He makes an overexaggerated frown.

"You work at the strip club now?" I tease. "What's your specialty dance move? The slut drop?"

"Ha, ha," he replies in a dry tone.

Crow wraps an arm around me. "Where are you off to with a pitcher of alcohol?"

"I was going to walk to Izzy's. It's just down the road, isn't it?"

"You don't even know where it is? Come on, I'll walk you over," Crow says, turning to Dee. "I'll be five minutes."

"I hope she's home," I say as we make our way by foot.

"She's always home," notes Crow, amusement in his tone. "She's probably sitting on her couch on her laptop, Shadow by her side."

"So you guys just drop in whenever you want to?"

"Exactly. What's family for?" Crow replies chirpily, moving out of the way when I accidentally spill some of the cocktail. "Shit, sorry."

We arrive at Izzy's house, and Crow knocks. We can hear Shadow at the door, barking his little head off. The door opens and she stands there in her pajamas, smiling at us. "Well, well, what do we have here? Come on in, guys."

"I'm just here to drop her off," Crow says, waiting for me to get inside. "Call me when you're done, I'll come and get you, all right? And lock up."

"Yes, sir," Izzy says, closing the door and turning to me. "What have I missed? Wait, let me get some glasses and salt so we can have one of those while you tell me."

I walk through her cute boho-style house, which is so beautifully decorated and instantly gives me a homey vibe, and end up in her kitchen where she pulls out two margarita glasses and dips the rims in salt before we pour my homemade margaritas into them. We sit in her living room, where her laptop is open and waiting, just as Crow predicted.

Shadow comes and sits next to me, brown eyes begging for attention, so I pat him with one hand and drink with the other.

"So the men are discussing their plan of action right now, but apparently some drug lord has been asking around about the Knights, and it's gotten back to us, and now we need to know why, and how this Palmer guy fits into the whole thing," I explain to Izzy, who sips on her cocktail with wide eyes.

"What the hell did we do to some drug lord?" she asks, confusion etched on her expression. "Why does this shit always happen to us?"

"I don't know. We need to figure out what the tie is between them and us," I state, looking down at Izzy's laptop. "We should do some research of our own. Let's see what comes up when we search."

We start online searching, and we find a man by the name of Grayson Palmer on social media.

"So it is his real name? Do you think this is even him? Maybe whoever told Renny about it gave his real name instead of his shady drug lord name," Izzy murmurs, flicking through his photos. "He looks like a normal guy. From his social media, it looks like he lives a relatively clean, boring life. Look, he even volunteers his time at the local food bank and donates there every week. He's older than I thought he would be."

"So he's a generous drug lord who cares about the community?" I say as we scan through the photos. "I don't know, are we sure this is him? His profile looks extremely wholesome."

"Well, he hasn't posted in like two years," Izzy says, shrugging. "Let's look at some older photos," she murmurs, going right to the bottom of the album and starting there.

She swipes through a few, and one of them catches my eye. "Wait, hold on, go back to that one."

She goes back, and looks at me expectantly. The photo is a group photo of five people, and I recognize the one in the middle.

I point to the woman standing next to Palmer, looking up at him with stars in her eyes.

"That's my mother."

Chapter Sixteen

"That's your mom?" Izzy asks, zooming in on the photo. "Are you sure?"

"I'm sure," I say, narrowing my eyes. "She's much younger, but yes, that's definitely her."

Izzy looks at me with wide eyes. What does this even mean?

"Maybe they're old high school friends or something," she suggests, wrinkling her nose. "I mean, come on, there has to be a valid explanation for this."

"Should I call her and ask? I don't know what to do right now. She's already hounding me to get my ass home, and if I ask her any questions she's going to worry even more about me." I groan, scrubbing my hand down my face in frustration.

"Of all the ties, I must admit I wasn't expecting this one," Izzy muses, taking a screenshot of the photo. "I don't think you should say anything to her yet. Let's speak to Temper and see what he says." She closes her laptop and chugs the rest of her drink. "I think we're going to need another one."

"Yes, please," I agree, sighing.

How the hell does Mom know some drug kingpin? My mom is the most innocent, boring woman I've ever known. She sticks to herself, she makes jars of jam and preserves in her spare time and I don't think I've ever seen her have a glass of wine, never mind have any kind of interest in drugs. Even though she owns and runs a bar, she's never been into drinking, or any other vices that I can think of.

My mind is blown right now.

We're tipsy...more like borderline drunk when Temper and Renny show up at the door.

"We have something to show you," Izzy says to Temper. We all sit down and we show them the picture.

"That's your mom?" Renny asks, looking between me and the photo. "You don't really look like her."

"I know," I reply, holding my phone. "What do we do? Do I call her and ask her or are we just going to leave it? This could mean nothing at all and be a huge coincidence or..."

Or like Izzy said, it's the unexpected connection that we've been looking for.

"Don't worry," Temper assures me, standing behind me and gently massaging my shoulders. "Whatever it is, we will sort it out, okay?"

I nod, but really all I want to do is speak to my mom.

We all head back to the clubhouse, even Izzy, who gives up on work to spend some extra time with us.

Even when life is going to shit, it's nice to have some people who are right there with you.

"Where are we going?" I ask Temper, staring out at the road, trying to see where the hell he is taking us.

"I told you, it's a surprise," he says again, giving me a quick grin. "You've been sitting in the clubhouse worrying about things since yesterday, and we need to get your mind off everything."

How do you get your mom being friends with a drug lord off your mind? It isn't lost on me that I may be the common denominator here, although I have no idea how.

I've decided that when I'm alone, I'm going to call her and get to the bottom of it. Drinking with Izzy last night didn't help and sitting in my room all day today overthinking didn't either. When Temper came into my room and told me to get ready because we were going somewhere, I wasn't exactly in the mood for it, but he insisted. I'm glad I listened to him, though, because sitting around feeling sorry for myself and the situation the MC and myself are in wasn't exactly being productive.

When we stop in front of a lake, I have to admit, that's not what I was expecting. "What are we doing here?"

He just smiles, gets out of the car and comes to open my door. "Let me show you."

We walk toward the water, and then Temper hands a man some money, a man who gives us his canoe in return.

"You ever done this before?" Temper asks, handing me a life jacket.

"Uhh, no," I say, putting it on, and then pick up one of the paddles. "What if it tips over?"

The water is extremely dark, and who knows what the hell could be down there?

"It won't," he promises. "And I can do the paddling if you want. You can just relax and enjoy the ride."

The man gives us a few instructions, and then helps us get into the canoe.

After that, we're on our own.

I'm not sure about this whole thing at the start—the paddling is harder than I thought it was going to be—but once we're out for a few minutes I start to relax and take in the breathtaking scenery in front of us.

"The water is like a mirror," I say to him from the front, where I'm sitting. All of the trees near the shore are reflected on the still water, and it's such a beautiful sight.

"I know, it's beautiful, isn't it? Like glass," he agrees, paddling skills much better than mine. "When you look down, it's kind of trippy, because it looks like the trees are underwater."

"Or like another dimension," I say, unable to look away. We paddle together for about an hour, seeing birds and simply enjoying the view before we turn the canoe back around.

"I like coming here when I need to think. You can stop paddling if you want," he says to me. "You relax. I can take care of it."

My brow furrows. "Are you telling me to stop paddling because it's easier for you if I don't?" I'll admit that every time I paddle, I go too far left or right and we almost hit the bank, but still, I'm putting in some effort and trying here.

I hear his laughter from behind me. "Maybe."

"Fine." I smirk, lifting my paddle up and letting him do all the work while I relax. "I have a blister on my hand anyway."

"Do you?" he asks, sounding concerned. "Definitely don't paddle then. I don't want you hurting your hands."

"It's fine," I say. I kind of feel like Pocahontas when

she's going down the river, singing "Just Around the Riverbend."

"We should play some music," I say out loud. "The *Pocahontas* soundtrack would be so good right now, don't you think?"

Temper is silent for a few moments, and then the song I was humming in my head is suddenly playing from his phone, and I feel like I'm in my own Disney movie, singing along loudly and wishing I had a talking raccoon with me.

"How did you know this was the song I was referring to?" I ask, turning around and looking at him.

"'Just around the riverbend,'" he sings, arching his brow like come on, it's obvious.

"I'm surprised you know this song at all."

"I have two nieces and a nephew, remember?" he fires back, singing along to the next few lines too. I'm not going to lie, I'm impressed. I never pictured a big biker like Temper to ever share a moment like this with me.

When we make it back to the shore, with people around, he still has the soundtrack playing. He doesn't care what people think, and I love that about him.

I also love that he pulls me out of my comfort zone and makes me do things that I never would have done otherwise. I get out of the canoe first, and wait for him to get out and pull the canoe up on the shore before I take off my life jacket.

"Thanks for bringing me here," I say. "It was honestly so amazing out there."

"You're welcome. Thank you for coming along with me, even though you had no idea what the hell we were doing," he says, winking at me. "At least I know that you trust me again now."

I roll my eyes. "Okay, okay, don't get ahead of yourself there, buddy."

He laughs and wraps his arm around me. "Come on, let's get something to eat."

He can do no wrong today.

When we get back to the clubhouse, Temper gets a call and says that he has to head out, but will be back later with dinner. So I decide to have a long shower, brush out my knotty canoe hair and get into my pajamas before calling my mom.

"Abbie? Are you okay?" is how she answers the phone, so my voice message clearly did nothing to ease her worry over me being gone.

"I'm fine," I reply, hesitating. "How's everything?"

"It will be better when you get home," she states, sighing. "I don't know what the hell is going on with you, Abbie, but you need to be home where you belong."

I try not to let her saying "where you belong" irk me.

"I told you I will be there soon," I say. "I'm actually calling because I have something to ask you."

"What is it?" she asks instantly. "If you want me to come and get you from somewhere, I can leave right now."

"No!" I say, a little too forcefully. "No, Mom, I don't want you to come and get me. I've told you that I'm fine. I'm not a little girl, I'm twenty-eight, and it's actually not a crime for me to be somewhere on my own."

"I know that," she huffs. "I'm just—"

"Worried, I know," I cut her off. "But I've told you a million times that I'm fine, happy even, and that I'll be home soon."

"What did you want to ask me then?"

"Who is Grayson Palmer, and how do you know him?" I ask, getting straight to the point.

She's quiet for a few seconds. "Why do you ask?"

"I saw a picture of you and him," I admit. "An old picture. And I just want to know what your connection is to this man."

Who apparently is a fucking drug lord.

Her long hesitation lets me know that she does know something about this man; she just doesn't want to tell me. If it wasn't a big deal, she would have just said *Oh, I knew him in high school, why?* or something along those lines, but she's acting sketchy as hell.

"Mom?"

When she starts crying, I'm wondering what the hell is going on.

"It's all my fault, Abbie. I'm so sorry. I panicked and called him."

"You called Palmer?" I ask, trying to make sense of this whole thing and why she's suddenly so upset.

"When Ivy said you were close to L.A., I called him because I know he lives there, and he used to be an old friend of mine. I asked him to find you, and to make sure that you're okay," she explains, sniffling. "Did he find you? What has happened?"

I open my mouth and close it a few times before I actually answer. "Let me get this straight. You were worried about me, so you called up your old friend, who is apparently a drug kingpin or whatever, and asked him to find me and check up on me to make sure I'm okay? You don't have any other friends who live near L.A.? Perhaps ones who aren't criminals?"

Little bit hypocritical of me, considering where I'm sitting right now, but still, come on.

She then has the audacity to come back at me with, "He's not a bad man. I mean, he wouldn't hurt you."

I feel like my life is currently full of men like that. Ones who aren't necessarily good, but are good to me. "I don't even know what to say right now."

She starts crying again before saying, "I had to call him, Abbie. He has connections. I didn't know what was going on with you, and I know you left with one of the bikers. I'm not stupid, I looked at the camera surveillance! I told you to stay away from them!"

"The bikers are my friends" is all I can think of to reply to that one with. "If you can be friends with a drug dealer, I can be friends with bikers."

She pauses, and then sighs. "He is your father."

And just like that, once again, my whole world changes.

Chapter Seventeen

I grew up without a dad, and because I never had one from the beginning, I didn't think much of it. Whenever anyone would ask about my father, I always replied that I didn't have one, that I only had a mother. I wouldn't say it in a sad way, it was just a fact.

Only when I got to about twelve did I ask about him, and my mom told me that he lived in California, and that we were all better off without him. Again, I didn't think much of it, just that he mustn't have wanted to be in my life, and that was it.

And now, after all of these years, she's dropping this bomb on me? After hanging up on her in shock, I've been lying in bed staring at the ceiling and just trying to make sense of all of this.

I left town without a word, and when she found out I was staying near L.A., the same city as the father I've never met, the one who didn't bother to be in my life or even send me a fucking birthday card once a year, she decided to call him, of all people, and ask him to find me and make sure I'm okay.

Now that I'm an adult and can take care of myself.

This is fucking rich.

At least I solved the puzzle and figured out why Palmer has been asking around about the MC: because

Mom knew I left with Temper, who she knows is the president of the Knights of Fury MC. She would have passed on that information to him.

I can't believe this.

Half of my DNA belongs to a drug dealer.

No, *the* drug dealer.

No wonder I was so drawn to Temper. I'm the daughter of a criminal.

I don't know how to break this news to everyone, because it's all kinds of fucked-up. How is the MC going to react to this? Temper has never asked anything about my dad, and I've never brought him up.

Really, it still hasn't changed anything.

I still don't have a dad.

Now, though, I know who my sperm donor is, and it's looking like I haven't won the genetic lottery.

Forcing myself out of bed, I drag my feet to the kitchen and pull out a bottle of vodka from the freezer, just as Crow walks in. His eyes widen as I start drinking it from the bottle, no chaser needed, because I currently feel like I'm dead inside. I can't even taste the vodka; I might as well be drinking water.

"Wow, what's going on, Abbie? Are you okay?" he asks, coming over and taking the bottle off me, and then he sets it down on the table. "I'm pretty sure anyone drinking liquor straight from the bottle is not okay. Do you want me to call Temper?"

"No, it's okay. No need to bother him," I say, sitting down at the table and looking into Crow's blue eyes. "Life is hard."

He nods. "Life is hard, yes. But you need to concentrate on the good things and say fuck you to the bad."

He gets up and gets two glasses and some lemonade,

then pours us both a drink. "Much more civilized," he murmurs as he slides it over to me.

"Thanks," I whisper, swallowing half the glass in one go.

"Come here," he says, pulling me against his chest and rubbing my back. "Whatever it is, it's going to be okay. You have us, and we will fix whatever it is, okay? Who has upset you? Do you want me to go and kick someone's ass?"

I smile against him, then start crying, because that's how fucking messed up my head is right now.

"What's wrong?" I hear Temper ask, panic in his tone. He comes over and pulls me away from Crow, lifting me up in his arms. "What happened?" he asks Crow, his voice now laced with fury. "I left her here with you for a few hours and she's fuckin' crying?"

"I don't know what's happened," Crow says, staying calm. "She came into the kitchen and was drinking straight vodka from the bottle when I found her, and I was just asking her what's wrong."

Temper's voice must have gotten everyone's interest, because suddenly the kitchen is filled with the MC. Saint, Renny, Dee and Chains, and all with their eyes on me.

"Get out of here!" Temper yells at them all, his booming voice scaring the shit out of me. I've never heard him use that tone before, and that volume, and it's like it came out of nowhere.

The men start to leave, but I say, "Wait."

They might be scared of Temper, but I'm not, and I know he'd never do anything to hurt me. He's angry for me, because I'm upset, and he wants them to give me space.

They all might as well know what's going on. They'd hear about it anyway.

"I found out why Palmer has been asking about the MC," I declare, looking at Temper's face.

"What are you talking about?" he asks, putting me down and cupping my cheek. "What has happened, Abbie?"

"I spoke to my mom, and she told him to come and find me," I explain. "Because apparently they're old friends."

"Okay, but why are you crying?" he asks, wiping my still wet cheeks. "Has he done something to you? Said something? Because I will fuckin' rip him apart with my bare hands if he has upset you."

"She also told me that he's my father," I blurt out, looking Temper right in the eye as fresh tears drop.

His eyes widen in realization, and he leads me out of the kitchen and into my room, closing and locking the door behind us.

"She told you that on the phone?" he asks, sitting down with me on the bed. "You never knew who your dad was?"

I shake my head and tell him the story from start to end.

"Come here," he says gently, and hugs me tightly. "I'm sorry you had to find out about who your father is this way. You know it's up to you what you do with this information, though, and you don't need to decide right now. But I'm here to help you no matter what, okay? I have your back. We all do. And that doesn't stop when you leave here. I'm always going to have your back."

"My father is a drug dealer," I say with no emotion. I've always wondered about him, and this is what he ended up being? "How the fuck is this my life?"

"You don't have to acknowledge him if you don't want to," Temper says, kissing the top of my head. "And you know none of us here are going to judge you. Hell, if anything you probably fit in better here now."

I laugh at that, wiping my face. "What are we going to do about him, though? If he comes here looking for me?"

"Whatever you want us to do," he replies in all seriousness. "We can kick his ass for not being there for you if you like. Or we can threaten him. Ask him to give you money. Whatever."

I shake my head. "I don't think any of that will be necessary."

"The option is there," he promises, lying down on the bed and pulling me down with him. "You can't choose your parents, unfortunately. My dad walked out on us all, and my mom died of an overdose. In front of us. So I get it."

"What?" I whisper, my heart breaking for him. "How old were you?"

"About five when Dad left, and ten when Mom died," he admits. "It was just me and Trade after that, and we took care of each other as much as we could. We got put into foster care."

"I'm so sorry," I say, kissing his cheek. "No wonder you're so tough."

He's been through so much, and from such a young age. I don't know what I've done for him to let me in, but I feel special that he's done so.

"I'm always here for you, too," I say, wanting him to know that this loyalty is a two-way street.

We lie like that together, just cuddling, until we both fall asleep.

I don't know how he always makes it feel like it's all going to be okay, but he does.

And I'm thankful for it.

Chapter Eighteen

I wake up feeling much better, and also a little embarrassed by my display of weakness last night in front of all the men. I was just so upset, I couldn't have contained it even if I tried. I know they won't hold any of it against me. It's just hard to face people who saw you in such a weak moment.

When I tell Temper this, he says, "Babe, you have no reason to be embarrassed. And trust me, the only thing they will be concerned about is you and if you're all right. No judgment in these walls, I promise you that."

First of all, he called me babe, which is cute, and secondly he's right, because as soon as I emerge from the room, all I get is love. Crow hugs me and tells me he's here if I need him. Saint, Dee and Renny come over and ask me if I'm okay. Skylar and Izzy bring flowers, chocolates and wine, and even Chains hugs me, and whispers into my ear, "I know where we can hide his body."

There's no judgment and no grudges held over my outburst. It honestly seems that no one cares who my dad is or what he does; they only care about me, and who I am, and it's such a nice feeling to know that.

I'm enough here.

And they have my back when I need them.

In this moment I can see why the men wanted to join the MC, and why the women love these men so much and stay here, loyal to them, even if on occasion it means that they have a target on their back.

It all makes sense why people choose this life.

Temper's right, you can't choose your family, but you can make your own, and that's exactly what they've done here.

And somehow I've become a part of it.

I don't know how it's happened, but I have, and now I don't want to get out of it. I don't want to leave.

"Maybe I should send him a message or something and tell him I'm here because I want to be and to stop looking for me," I say to Temper, out of nowhere, my mind unable to let this whole Palmer thing go.

We've realized Mom called him after the first shooting, so I know the mercenaries aren't connected to him, but I don't want him to bring on any more trouble to the club on my behalf. They have enough on their plate right now.

"I don't know if that will work," Temper admits, glancing up from his phone. "He might think we made you do it, who knows? But we can try it, if that's what you want to do. Do you want to speak to him, though? If you don't, we can always handle it for you."

"No, this is my problem," I say. "I need to handle it. I can't hide from him forever, and it's my fault he's poking around the MC anyway."

Temper nods. "Okay. I don't like it, for the record. But I said we'd handle it however you wanted to, and I meant that."

"I appreciate that," I tell him, smiling. "I know how

rare it is for you to give up control, and how you're used to making decisions without being questioned."

He throws his head back and laughs. "Even the president of an MC has to be taken down a notch now and again, hey? And I think you're the only woman who gets to do that."

"Well, we have to be on an even playing field, after all," I say, reaching over and taking his hand in mine. "Which means sometimes, more often than not, I get to have my way."

He laughs again. "Unless it comes to your safety; then I'll override that."

I roll my eyes and give his hand a squeeze. "I'm safe. I'm surrounded by a bunch of cavemen and the two most badass women I've ever met."

"You're badass too," he says, pulling me out of my chair and onto his lap. "You've adapted like a queen, Abbie. We've thrown you into some pretty fucked-up situations, yet here you are, smile on your face and throwing sass around. You're a strong woman, you know that? I'm proud of you."

"Thanks," I say, ducking my head.

I know that in the short time I've been here I've grown as a person, and that has been because of these situations and how far I've been pushed out of my comfort zone. I'm just going to keep getting stronger, and I know that.

And I'm proud of that.

I'm becoming who I was always meant to be.

The woman my mom has always tried to pull me back from, because she didn't want the world to hurt me in any way. What she doesn't realize is that being fearful of life is only barely living, and sometimes the gamble is worth it. Yeah, I can get hurt, physically, emotionally even.

But living, I mean truly living? There's nothing like it. And it's worth anything that might happen.

Living without fear, it's exhilarating.

"Who knew this is where I'd be?" I think out loud. "Just because I said yes to a date with a man I've had a crush on for years."

Temper holds the back of my neck. "I don't know if that's a good thing or not. A few hours spent with me and I brought you back down the rabbit hole with me."

I close my eyes and rest my head against him. "It is what it is. We can't change what has happened; all we can do is push forward and learn from each setback."

"Spoken like a true Knight," he says, smile in his tone. "What can we teach you next? You want to learn how to ride a motorcycle? Kick a grown man's ass in a fight?"

"I don't know about the motorcycle thing, but I'd like to learn some self-defense, for sure." Anything that makes me less of a victim.

"That we can do," he says, stroking his calloused fingers up and down my bare arms. "We'll have you boxing in no time."

Ivy messages me about the whole Palmer thing. We've always known that we have different dads, because I've met hers. He used to come around when we were children, but then he moved overseas, and all she gets now is the occasional birthday and Christmas phone call.

Ivy: How are you doing? I'm here for you if you want to talk about it. I can't believe Mom has handled this situation like this, and knew who your dad was all along. I'm so angry at her, Abbie. I can't imagine how you must be feeling right now. Just know that I love you, and I've got your back.

Abbie: Thank you. I'm feeling pretty shitty, but it is what it is. I can't wait to see you. I miss you so much! I'm being looked after here, though, so you don't need to worry about me.

"I wish Ivy could come out here and experience L.A. with me. She'd love it, especially the food and the shopping," I say to Temper. I do feel guilt over the fact I'm enjoying life while she's busting her ass for me. I love how the MC lives close to L.A, though, close enough to enjoy the big city benefits, but they also have their own quiet little nook in their own town.

"We can make that happen," he promises, tucking my hair back behind my ear.

"When the timing is right." I sigh, closing my eyes.

"Yeah, shit is going to get hectic around here. We've got two new prospects joining soon, and Crow and Chains will become full patched members. I want to get our numbers up so we can become a stronger force," he explains. "But at the same time I want only men who we can trust, who can be loyal to us. I'd rather have a few loyal men over hundreds of disloyal men."

He smiles and adds, "Just like I've always wanted just one loyal woman. Quality over quantity."

"Which doesn't really match up with the whole biker reputation," I tease, running my fingers along his stubble. I like touching him, all the time, and I love that we're becoming so comfortable and affectionate with each other every single day. I've never really been some-one who wanted a boyfriend—or saw the appeal, if I'm being honest—but now I can see how some people be-come infatuated with their other half. I know Temper and I aren't officially a couple, and we might never go further than what we are now, and this, but he's still always going to mean something to me. I'm going to have no regrets about what we have.

"You can't believe all the stereotypes," he replies, brown eyes dancing with amusement. "I'm glad you took a chance on me. And I hope that even through all of this bullshit, I'm worth it to you. Because I'm telling you right now: I'd go to hell and back for you, Abbie."

Saint comes to speak to Temper before I'm able to reply to that. "We found one of the men who attacked us at the front of the nightclub. Renny has eyes on him right now. He's at a hotel downtown."

Temper stands with me in his arms, then puts me down and gives me a long, deep kiss. "Stay here. I'll be back."

"Wait," I say, reaching out for him before he follows Saint back inside.

He turns and says, "I'll leave Crow here with you. Skylar and Izzy will be coming here, too. I want you all together so we know you're here and safe." He leaves without another word.

I sit back down in his chair, and Crow soon joins me, bringing a pack of cards with him. "The girls are on their way," he says, sitting down next to me and shuf-fling the pack. "And then I'm going to lock the place up—no one is getting in or out until the men return."

"I hate sitting here just waiting," I say, but I know I wouldn't be much help to them. "What are they going to do anyway? Kidnap the guy and torture him for information?"

Crow's blue eyes go wide, and his hands still mid-shuffle. "You've got an evil mind, you know that? I'm sure that they're just going to ask the nice man some friendly questions."

I roll my eyes. "Yeah, I've seen the type of friendly you all are."

"Hey, both times we've been shot at, we haven't started any shit. Not yet anyway. We're the innocent ones here, think about it," he says with a smirk. "And you've been there both times, maybe you're the one bringing this all on us."

"Very funny," I growl, scowling. "I'm only here right now because I was in the wrong place at the wrong damn time."

"Some good came from it, though," he says softly, giving me the side eye. "We can all see how happy you both are."

"I am happy," I admit. "But that doesn't mean this whole situation isn't complicated. I don't know how you stay so chirpy, Crow, but this life is stressful."

"Stressing isn't going to help any," he replies, dealing me some cards. "I need to stay calm, because if I'm not, I'm not going to think straight. And that could cost someone their life."

"If only it was as easy as that," I grumble. "What are we playing?"

"Omi."

"What's Omi?" I ask, brow furrowing. "I've never heard of it." I pick up the four cards that he dealt me and look at them.

"It's a Sri Lankan card game my ex-girlfriend taught

me," he explains, then gives me a rundown of all the rules. "We need four players though, so we need to wait for the other two, but if you already know what's going on, then it will be easier to teach them."

Skylar and Izzy arrive, and Crow locks up the clubhouse while we sit outside and chat. "What do you think is happening right now?" I ask them. "In broad daylight. What do you think their plan is?"

"Follow the man until they find the right opportunity," Skylar guesses, staring at her short black nails. "That's what I'd do. He might even lead them to the rest of the men. Don't worry, Abbie, this isn't their first rodeo. They know what they're doing. It just means a long day of waiting for us."

"But if they didn't know where we were, in the back of their minds they'd be worrying," Izzy explains, and sighs heavily. "Just means we also need to not worry, and keep busy so the time goes faster."

"Crow is going to teach us a card game," I say, glancing toward the kitchen window. "I'm guessing we shouldn't have wine, in case we need our wits about us, but I'll get some soda and snacks, so we can pretend we're all just here to hang out."

And not that our men are currently staking out a mercenary, who has tried to kill us all twice.

How is this my life?

Chapter Nineteen

"This card game is the shit," Skylar announces about an hour later. "It's luck, skill and bluffing all in one game."

We are in two teams, and you sit diagonal from your teammate. It's me and Crow against Skylar and Izzy.

"I know, why are we only learning this game now?" I agree, playing my ace of hearts and grinning. Crow keeps checking his phone, making sure the men aren't trying to contact him. They've been silent so far, which is kind of annoying because an update would be nice, but we're all trying to just make the best out of the moment.

"Where's your sister and Mila?" I ask Izzy, wondering why they aren't here.

"They're with Trade," she explains. "They are looking for a bigger house so they can all move in together. Safe to say I'll be so sad to see them go, especially Mila."

"Are you going to finally move into the clubhouse?" Crow asks, studying her. "Or are you going to keep giving Renny a heart attack by refusing to leave your house, even though you're going to be in there alone?"

"The latter," she admits, laughing. "I love my house—it's my own little slice of heaven. I could never get any work done here, there's always people here and shit going down. And I'm literally down the road, with fancy-ass security and a dog. I'm fine. Renny basically lives at my house anyway."

"That's true," Crow admits, placing down the final trump card and winning the game. "And Abbie, we win again."

"Dammit!" Skylar calls out, shaking her fist in the air. "I demand a rematch."

"Temper sent a message," Crow says, quickly grabbing his phone off the table as it beeps. "They're all good, still following him. Hopefully this guy leads them to his house or something, or meets up with the other men, or his boss, and we can put this whole scenario to rest."

We all share a look.

"This could go on into the night," he adds, which is exactly what I was about to say. "Maybe we should sort out some food, and put some movies on or something."

"*Harry Potter* marathon?" I suggest to them. Harry always makes things better.

"Sounds good to me," Izzy says, standing up and stretching her arms above her head. "I'm guessing we can't order food in, so we're going to have to make do with what we have in the cupboard."

"Temper stocked the fridge and cupboards," I say, grinning. "So we have plenty to work with. I can make dinner if you like."

"We'll all help," Skylar says, winking at me. "Come on, it will keep us all busy. And I'm getting hungry."

We cook dinner, eat, and then watch *Harry Potter* until we all fall asleep.

With none of them home yet.

* * *

I wake up to Temper lifting me off the couch and carrying me not to my bed, but his. I've barely been inside his room, because we always seem to hang around in mine, so it's nice being in his space, even though our rooms basically look the same.

"What happened?" I ask, yawning. "What time is it? Did you only just get home?"

"It's six a.m., and yes, we just got in. I had a shower then came to get you," he says, pulling the blankets down and laying me on the mattress. He jumps in and pulls the covers over us. "We followed him all night until he finally met up with some familiar faces."

"And? What happened?"

"Nothing, we let him go, for now," he admits, kissing my cheek.

"What? Why?" I ask, brow furrowing.

All of that and they let him go? What am I missing here?

"It got a little more complicated than we thought," he says quietly, sighing. "We saw Georgia with them. And we need to play this the right way, because this woman gets away every damn time, mainly because none of us can touch her."

"Why not?" I ask, frowning. "Who is she?"

"Because she's Skylar's mother," he says, grimacing. "And she used to be Hammer's old lady. I know her well, and because of who she is, none of us can go through with what we should have done a long time ago."

I stay silent, because surely he can't mean what I think he does.

At the end of the day, the woman is still Skylar's mother.

"What does Skylar say?" I ask.

"That's why we didn't make any moves tonight. We need to speak with her and formulate a plan. The thing is, we know where Georgia lives with her husband, so we'll always be able to find her. And it's clear she's never going to let this vendetta against us go. She's going to want to bring us down until the day she dies."

"What a mess this is," I whisper, running my hands down his bare back. "I'm glad you are all safe."

"Worried about me, were you?" he asks, kissing me again.

"Of course I was, especially when you weren't home by midnight," I say, and kiss his lips, then his jawline and his neck.

He makes a growling sound that turns me on, and gives me the confidence to explore his body a little in the sunlight. I kiss him down his chest, taking my time and teasing him, glancing up and looking him right in the eyes before continuing. I love listening to him, the hitches in his breath, his hand in my hair, stroking me, encouraging me.

Pulling down his boxer shorts, I find him already hard, but he gets harder the second my hand touches him and begins to stroke. Up and down, up and down, I get a feel for him before I taste him with my lips, my tongue licking over the head of his cock, and then sliding him into my mouth as far as I can without choking.

"Fuck," he grits out, teeth clenched. His hips arch slightly, like he's unable to keep still, while I continue to lick and suck. My nails score down his thighs, and he makes another growling sound. I don't know how much longer he's going to wait and let me play, I feel like he's on the edge, and wanting to take control.

"I'm going to come," he says, brown eyes pinned on me.

I know he's giving me the option to move away but I decide not to. I'm curious, and this will be yet another first for me. He tries to move away, but I place my palms down on his hips so he can't escape, and suck harder.

It works, and he comes in my mouth, but now I don't know what to do—do I swallow it, or run and spit it out? The latter seems like the easier option, so I head to the bathroom and wash my mouth out. But then I realize the taste is already there, so I probably should have just swallowed.

Stepping back in the bedroom, Temper lies there naked, with his arms back behind his head. I join him back in bed and rest my cheek against his chest, while his fingers run down my bare back.

He kisses the top of my head, then rolls me to my back. "My turn."

I take a deep breath as he teases me, paying special attention to my breasts before dropping lower, kissing down my stomach, around my navel, then lower still. When he nibbles on my inner thighs, I moan out loud, and when he puts his mouth on my pussy, I can't help the sounds that I make. He takes his time with me, in no rush, my orgasm building, and my desire taking control of all of my senses.

In this moment, nothing other than him and my pleasure matters.

And when I orgasm, sparks fly, and my body comes apart and then rejoins. Even after that, it's not over—he slides his cock inside of me, thrusting a few times before pulling out and going back down on me. He then flips me on my stomach, lifting my hips up, my ass pushed out in the air, and he licks my pussy from behind.

I hold on to the headboard for dear life, my thighs trembling. I thought I'd feel shy, or maybe even want to cover up, but I feel safe and am just enjoying every new damn thing he does to me. He's giving me a taste of what I've been missing out on, but at the same time making me so glad I waited for someone I feel comfortable with to explore my sexuality.

He makes me come one more time before he slides back into me and thrusts until he finishes. I fall forward on the bed, a smile on my face, sated and happy. Temper pulls me back with him, so he's spooning me from behind, then kisses the back of my neck.

"I love you," he says, exhaling deeply.

I swallow hard. "I love you too, Temper."

Which means we're both fucked.

Chapter Twenty

"I can't believe this shit," Skylar groans, shoulders hunched in defeat. "It just makes no sense. Hammer is gone—why can't she let the Knights be now? I just don't understand why she hates me so much."

After breaking the news to her about her mom being involved in all of this, we all sit around in the living room, trying to be there for her as she processes this. I personally don't see what kind of solution there could be. It seems like Georgia's never going to let this go—she means to hold this grudge against the MC until she dies.

It seems the woman really doesn't take rejection well.

From what I've heard, Georgia is the Knights' nemesis, a friend turned enemy, and she's never going to just go away. It seems like she has made it her life's work to bring the MC down, and that she has tried over and over again to bring pain and harm to anyone, including her own daughter, who calls this clubhouse home.

"I think she pictured herself being the queen bee around here for the rest of her life," Temper states, arms crossed against his broad chest.

"And now she's never going to be," Renny adds, looking at me.

Clearing my throat, I glance back at Skylar. "I'm sure she doesn't hate you. She's obviously not thinking straight. I don't think you should take this as a personal hit. She clearly wants the MC taken down, and you just happen to be a part of that."

"I agree," Saint says, arm around his woman. "She's not right in the head, Skylar. She has some vendetta against us, and it's clear she's not letting it go. She knows that we won't hurt her because she's your mother, and now she's playing that card yet again, thinking that we won't do any damage."

"So what do we do?" Skylar asks him.

"Damage," Saint replies, baring his teeth. "I say we speak to her husband and show him proof of the person she really is for a start. If she wants to try to ruin our lives, it's time for her to get a little payback. She's been playing dirty this whole time while we've been playing by the rules. Time to even the playing field."

"If we bring Neville into this, that's going to push her over the edge," Temper states, glancing around the group. "Are we all ready for the fallout?"

"She started this war," Renny adds, lips tight. "It's time we finished it."

Skylar ducks her head, but she doesn't disagree.

I don't envy the position she's in. Georgia sounds like a rotten person, but at the end of the day that's still her mom. I can't say what I'd do if I were in her situation.

Her family is coming after her family, and it's so fucked-up.

"She's not going to give up," she finally says. "She's going to keep coming after the club. She got Dad killed. I'm never going to forgive her for that, and I don't want to lose anyone else. My family is here now."

Temper gets a text message and he instantly stands. "All right, I have to go." He leans down and kisses me deeply. "I'll be back in a few hours."

He walks away, leaving everyone staring at me.

"What?" I ask them.

"Temper's into PDA now," Saint muses, a look of confusion on his face. "Fuckin' hell, anything is possible."

I ignore their needling and reply to my text messages from Mom and Ivy. Mom is asking me to forgive her, and that she should have been honest with me from the start about my dad. Ivy is asking me to bring her back something cool, and I appreciate the normalcy of her conversation over the deep one with Mom.

The conversation I had with Temper about contacting Grayson nags at me. With everything coming out about Skylar's mom's involvement, I think we could use as much help as we can get. And Palmer is a drug lord or kingpin, whatever terminology he prefers. Maybe he can help.

So I send my mother a message.

Abbie: Send me his number.

She's the one who brought him into this so quickly; she won't mind us having contact now. While I don't want any type of relationship with him, he may be able to help. These people, this family, they're worth it.

She takes an hour before she sends me his number; knowing her, she probably made up a pros and cons list or something like that. I type out a new message to Palmer.

Abbie: This is Abbie. You don't need to try to find me, I'm fine and I'll be back home before the week is over. Mom made a mistake trying to contact you. But since she did, I could use your help. Think you can crawl out from the rock you've been hiding under?

I hit send.

Hating that I keep checking my phone to see if he replies, I hide it under my pillow and try to keep myself busy. It's annoying he's affecting me—even though I'm trying hard to just pretend like nothing has changed, it clearly has. After all of these years, I have a face for my father, which makes it so much more real. It was easier before when I didn't have any information and I could just pretend I was created by immaculate conception or something like that. Now the bastard is living in my head, and I hate that he has a place there when he doesn't deserve it. If he doesn't reply to me, then I'll know once and for all what a waste of a human he is.

"Is everything okay?" Skylar asks, knocking on my door and coming in.

"I should be asking you the same thing," I say, tapping the spot next to me on my bed. "Parents can be so shitty, can't they?"

"You can say that again," she grumbles, sitting down and glancing around my room. "The worst part is that I'm so much closer to my brothers now, and I don't want something to happen that's going to tear us apart, you know? And if something happens to Mom and that's on me, they're going to hate me."

"It's such a hard situation," I whisper, squeezing her hand. "I'm sure there's a solution that doesn't involve her…going missing or anything. Maybe we can think of a way that gets her off our backs for good, but she remains alive and well?" I say it with hope, but deep down I don't know if that's realistic. She's out to kill the MC and she put her own daughter in danger, sending men to attack them when she was there. Skylar could've been killed.

"That's what we've been trying to do this whole time." She sighs. "And it's why she keeps coming back, because we keep thinking we can fix this. But this problem never goes away. She's like a fucking boomerang— she just keeps coming back to fuck with us."

"I don't know what's going to happen, but I do know it will be okay," I promise, smiling sadly.

"I'm so glad you came into our lives, Abbie," she says, leaning over and giving me a kiss on my cheek. "You're the gentleness we needed here, but you're also so strong. It's so beautiful to see you and Temper together. You bring out the best in him, you know that? You soften him, and he hardens you."

"I'm pretty sure I'm meant to be hardening him," I joke.

She laughs and winks. "I've seen the way he looks at you."

Feeling my cheeks heat, I lift up my pillow and pick up my phone. "I've been avoiding checking this because I messaged Palmer, and I don't know if he's going to reply or not."

"Do you want to check together?" she asks.

I nod. "Okay."

We both hold the phone, my right hand her left, and I open my messages.

Sperm Donor: I'll help, but I just ask one thing…

I watch the three dots blink as he writes another message.

Sperm Donor: Come meet me in person.

Skylar and I share a look. "Is he seriously blackmailing me right now? The piece of shit."

"What are you going to do?" she asks, frowning. "Maybe he just wants to see you in person. Imagine having a child and you don't even know what she really looks like or anything. He might just want to meet you once and for all. You know, I was in a similar situation as you—my mom never told me who my dad was, and when I found out it was already too late, he was already dead."

"I'm sorry to hear that," I say, thinking about her words. I don't really know the full story on what happened between him and my mom. I deserve to know the truth and why he's been absent from my life. "I think I need to go. If he can help us, I can give him the face time. And as much as I want to think he's a scumbag loser who abandoned his child, I really don't know the whole story and I'm not sure I would believe anything my mother told me at this point. Is it wrong for me to go and ask him?"

"No. And if I were you, I'd go," she admits, rubbing my back. "Abbie, I think it's incredibly brave of you to open up this wound to help the MC. It tells me that you are the perfect woman for Temper."

I smile. "Thanks. And I think you're right, but I should probably talk to Temper first."

If I'm going to be the queen around here, it's time I make some sacrifices of my own.

Chapter Twenty-One

When Temper returns, Skylar has me in the gym, teaching me a few self-defense moves, the rest of the MC around us in a circle. Crow taught me how to punch properly, and now I'm being taught how to get out of certain holds if someone tries to grab me. Using the technique Skylar showed me, I twist her arm and escape her hold from behind.

"Perfect." She beams, panting a little. "Man, I forgot how tiring this was. You want to take over, Prez?"

Temper nods, and steps into the circle and hands me some gloves. "Let's see what you got."

"You sure you want me to beat you in front of all your men?" I tease, sliding them on and holding my fists up in position, in front of my face. I start to weave and duck, putting on a little show for him.

He simply grins, flashing his teeth. "I'm sure I'll manage."

I can't deny being kind of turned on right now, especially with the way he's looking at me, like he wants to eat me alive. He puts on his own gloves and takes a similar stance, only he doesn't look like an idiot when he does it. He looks powerful, like a worthy opponent for anyone.

"You ready?" he asks, amusement in his gaze.

"Yes," I reply, making the first move forward and delivering the first punch. Like I imagined, he doesn't actually try to hit me. Instead he playfully makes a few jabs, but none of them connect, and he spends his time blocking my hits. "Come on, you're not going to break me."

"I'm not going to hit my woman," he says, smirking. "I just want to see what skills you have."

"And?"

"Workable," he replies, throwing his gloves on the floor, and lifts me in the air by my hips. "You're quick and determined. And fuckin' beautiful."

"I don't think that would distract many other people, just you." I grin, kissing his lips as he lowers my body down his.

"Um, we're still all here, guys," Skylar calls out, laughing. "Should we leave?"

"I feel like we should leave," Saint agrees, and they all do just that.

"Are we that bad to be around?" I ask Temper, laughing to myself and removing my gloves. "Oh yeah, while you were gone, I did a thing."

"What thing did you do?" he asks, lifting his chin and arching his brow.

"I messaged Palmer," I admit, telling him about the exchange.

"What are you going to do?" he asks, putting away the boxing gloves and taking my hand in his. "If you want to meet him, you know I'm coming, right? I mean, I can wait in the car or something, or hide out somewhere, but I'm going to be around in case he pulls some bullshit."

"I know," I say, lip twitching. "And yes, I want you to come with me, of course. I wouldn't do it without you."

"Okay, when do you want to meet him?" he asks, leading me outside.

"I'll message him now and say tomorrow? Do you have anything then?" I ask.

"Nothing that can't be moved."

Great.

Tomorrow, I meet my father.

Chapter Twenty-Two

I'm glad when Palmer chooses a public café, because I don't know how anything can go too wrong here. There's plenty of people around, and Temper is in a car at the front of the café, Saint at the back, and Renny down the road just in case. We don't know what he has planned, but we can never be too careful.

He's there before me, sitting alone with a coffee in front of him. I recognize him instantly from his social media—older, fit, with salt-and-pepper hair. The sound of the chair scraping as I pull it out makes him notice me.

"Abigail," he says, eyes widening as he takes me in. "You came."

"I did," I reply, sitting down. "I don't know why you wanted to see me, but here I am."

"Why would I not want to see my only child?" he asks, brow furrowing. "Just because I haven't been in your life doesn't mean that I don't care about you."

Lips tightening, I say nothing to that. The waitress comes over, and I order myself coffee.

Palmer leans forward and lowers his voice. "When your mom said that you had gone missing and left with the president of the Knights of Fury MC, of course I was worried. Why are you with them?"

He then slides me a note.

It reads: *If they're listening to this conversation so you can't say anything and you need me to help you, scratch your nose now.*

I blink slowly and shake my head. "I don't need any help, and I mean that. I wasn't being forced to say I'm okay when I'm not. I'm genuinely okay, and I will be going home soon."

"Okay." He nods, brows drawn together in confusion. "So you're willingly hanging around bikers?"

"Yes," I say, sighing. "I am. And I'm fine. So you don't need to ask around about them, and you can report back to Mom that you saw me and that I am indeed fine. They've done nothing wrong, and you don't need to start any shit with them."

"I want no trouble with the Knights. I just wanted to make sure that you were safe." He pauses, and then adds, "And I don't want any trouble with you, either."

"We don't have any problems here," I reply, eyes narrowing slightly. "I mean, I'm still in shock my father isn't exactly working a nine-to-five job, but it is what it is."

"I'm a legitimate businessman, Abbie," he assures me, not flinching.

"Just on paper?" I press, rolling my eyes.

"I'm surprised by your judgment, with the company you keep," he fires back. He looks like he wants to say something else, his mouth opening and closing, but then he shakes his head and sighs.

"You're beautiful...you have my eyes," he says, smiling sadly into his coffee. When he looks into my eyes, I'm shook. It's like I'm looking into a mirror. I was so mad at him when I came in, I haven't really looked at him.

I'm still staring when he continues, "I just had to make sure that you were okay."

"I want the story. I want to know why this is the first time I'm meeting you and why up until a few days ago, I thought my father's name was Cohen Pierce."

"Cohen Pierce is my birth name," he admits. "A name I don't go by anymore, and haven't in a long time. Your mom is the only one who still calls me that name."

I nod. "Why am I only meeting you now?"

He grimaces, and I'm not sure if he's going to answer me honestly or not. "It's complicated... When are you going to go home?" he asks, studying me.

"Soon," I reply. "There's a few things happening, things I don't want to bring home with me."

"What kind of things?" he asks, frowning. "What have you gotten yourself into?"

I hesitate before telling him. I don't know if I'm going to regret this or not, but it can't get any worse, right? "There are some guys after the MC, and for some reason they seem to have targeted me. And I'm trusting you to not tell Mom about this, please. I don't need her calling me and having an anxiety attack."

"I won't say a word to her," he assures me. "Wait. Who is after the MC?"

"Hired men. Mercenaries. At first we thought you hired them, but my mom told me she only called you after they attacked us. Twice. Umm...that's sort of why I'm here..."

He looks at me curiously.

I take a deep breath. "I don't know if I want to know what your business dealings involve or who your associates are, but do you think you can help?"

Grayson's eyes pop out. I can't tell if he's surprised

by what I asked him or by the fact that I actually asked for his help. "Do you know who hired them?"

I nod. "Yep. My friend's mother. Skylar's mother hates us, and wants to end us, basically. I have an enemy and she's out to get me."

His brows draw together. "Skylar?"

I nod again. He looks confused and I would be too. What normal people have mothers who hire people to kill your family? I decide to end the conversation here. Even though he's a kingpin, I'm sure he didn't expect his illegitimate daughter coming into his life asking for help from people trying to kill her and her friends. "So can you help?"

"Abbie... I—I mean, I don't know. I don't think this is a good idea. There's something you should probably know—"

All I hear is no. "You know what? Never mind. I better get going. Temper is in the car, just in case you tried to kidnap me or something." Not knowing what to do, I offer him my hand. He takes it and we awkwardly shake. "It was nice finally meeting you."

"You too, Abbie."

He looks like he wants to say more, but I get up and leave, feeling overwhelmed with the whole experience.

When I get back into the car, I can see Temper is visibly relieved. I tell him what he said, and even he seems surprised. "So he just wanted to make sure you were okay?"

"Yep. And I'm as surprised as you are. I was expecting some type of bullshit to go down, but no, he genuinely thought you guys were keeping me against my will and forcing me to say that I was okay."

"Our reputation must be really shit if a drug dealer is concerned," he mutters, and I have to agree.

Is this the last time I'm ever going to see this man? I don't know, but for now I'm just going to leave it as it is. I never needed him growing up, and I sure as hell don't need him now.

"He wouldn't help," I say to myself. "I asked and he said no." I don't know what I was thinking. Why would he want to get involved and jeopardize his operation over little ol' me? His daughter.

Temper grabs my hand and squeezes it. "Our time together is running out," he says, risking a glance at me before bringing his eyes back to the road. "Do you know how long you're going home for? I mean, are you going to come back? I will come and visit you every chance I can get...if you want me to."

We haven't had this conversation yet, but it's about time we discussed it all. I have no idea what's going to happen when I leave, which is probably why I've just been in denial and trying not to think about it. I don't want to lose him, and I do want to make this work. I just don't know how.

"I don't know," I admit. "I mean, of course I want to still be with you, and for us to try to see each other when we can, but I don't know when I *can* come back. I need to make sure Mom and Ivy are sorted, and that they can manage Franks without me."

"Once that is all sorted out, you could always finish your law degree here," he says. "I'm going to be honest, Abbie: I want you here. In an ideal world, you'd be here with me, living with me, being my old lady. The distance thing is going to be shit, but I want to make it work with you. Whatever it takes."

Whatever it takes.

"We can make it work," I say, smiling. "As long as we're both dedicated to doing so, we can make it happen, I know it. But yeah, it's going to be hard to leave you. Not going to lie."

He exhales deeply. "Can't tell you how glad I am that you're not running off and never looking back."

Laughing softly, I ask, "Did you really think that I'd do that?"

"After all the shit I've put you through? I don't know," he admits. "Maybe you'd decided to settle down with a banker or something, someone with a nine-to-five and some stability. Someone who you won't have to worry about every time they leave the house."

"Where's the fun in that?" I tease, grinning and squeezing his hand.

I can't deny that the thought has entered my mind, but there's only one Temper.

And he's mine.

Chapter Twenty-Three

"This is where she lives?" I ask Skylar the next day, eyes going wide in surprise. We decided we'd drive out to have a chat with Neville, to see if we can get some inside information on what's going on, anything that can help us and get us a step ahead of Georgia. When I was told that she lives out in the country, for some reason I wasn't expecting some cute-ass farm. I imagined whoever lives here to be wholesome farmers, dressed in overalls or something, not Hammer's ex–old lady, but here we are.

"Yeah, I know. She even gardens and shit," Skylar replies, turning to Temper. "So, I'm going to go in and speak to Neville, see what he knows about where she is, and then tell him that his wife is a psychotic socio-path who has hired a bunch of hit men to kill my family, probably with his money?"

"Exactly," Temper replies, not batting an eyelash.

"You sure you don't want me coming in with you?" Saint asks for the third time. "I don't know how I feel about this, Sky. Just let me come, say you wanted to introduce me to your stepdad or something."

"You'd intimidate him," she says, frowning. "I need him to be comfortable to tell me the truth, and to believe what I tell him. You standing there next to me, being all big and badass, isn't going to work in our favor. Besides, we're pretty sure Georgia isn't here, and Neville wouldn't harm a fly. He has always been much nicer to me than she was and has always made me feel welcome here at the farm. I want to make sure he's okay with everything that's going on as well. It must be a pretty shitty feeling to realize the woman you married and loved is actually a monster."

"Fine." He sighs. "The second anything feels off, you're out of there. And if you're not back in twenty minutes, I'm coming in."

"Fine," she agrees, kissing him, and then hops out of the car and speed walks to the front door.

I don't know what they hope to get out of this, but I'm intrigued to see how it goes. "Is this a good idea?" I ask Temper.

"We just need to test the waters and see what information we can get from Neville," he explains, lifting my hand to his lips and kissing my knuckles. "Don't stress, she will be fine. From what we've heard from Skylar, Neville is actually a really nice guy; he's nothing like Georgia."

"How can he be nice if he's with someone so evil?" I ask, glancing at the farmhouse and waiting for Skylar to reappear.

"She puts on a good show," Saint says from the back seat. "I'm talking Oscar-worthy performances. She's the master manipulator. I don't think you'd believe it until you see it for yourself."

"Intelligent and crazy isn't a good mix," Temper adds, his eyes never leaving the door that Skylar disappeared through. "She also looks extremely approachable and friendly, like a little petite, mother-type figure."

And I thought I had parent issues. The fact that Skylar turned out how she did even with a mother like that is a true testament to her character. She's amazing, and she should be so proud of herself to have become such a strong, kind woman even though she didn't have that example.

Twenty minutes pass, and Saint is about to leave the car to retrieve her when she walks back through the door. He gets out, opens the door for her, and kisses her as she reaches him.

"How did it go?" he asks her after she closes the car door.

"She doesn't live here anymore," she tells us, shaking her head. "Her and Neville aren't together at all and haven't been for a few weeks now. She emptied their joint bank accounts and left him."

"Holy shit. So he saw her true colors when it was too late," Saint adds.

"Yeah, and he's pissed," she says as we start to drive back home. "He was upset, but more pissed than anything. I never saw him angry, but I guess if my spouse cleaned out my bank accounts and left me and then I hear that she hired people to kill someone with that money, I guess I'd be angry too." She shrugs.

"Savage," Temper mutters under his breath.

"I mean, we all know what she's capable of, and in the big scheme of all the terrible things she's done this doesn't even make the top five. But fuck, it was hard seeing Neville like that. He didn't deserve that—he's been nothing but kind, loving and generous to her." Skylar sighs.

"It's not on you," Saint assures her. "You've done nothing wrong, and I know you feel bad for him, but come on. He was an idiot to stay with her for so long. He had to have sensed something was off with her. Not that it justifies anything she did—she's a totally evil person—but you have no reason to feel guilty."

"I know," she replies. "What are we going to do now?"

"Well, now we know she's living back in the city," Temper says. "Which means the last few weeks she's been right in our backyard, planning fuck knows what, which makes her more dangerous than we realized. We need to find out where she's living, and what the hell we're going to do to get her to back off. She's got money, and no Neville to hold her back now. She doesn't even have to bother with the nice girl act."

"Yeah, and now she doesn't have him distracting her," Skylar adds. "She literally has nothing to do with her time other than be an evil bitch, sitting there with her stolen money. I can just picture her now. I bet she's living it up in some fancy hotel, or already trying to get with another guy. Someone who has connections and isn't afraid to get his hands dirty."

"Someone who can help her take us down." Temper nods, agreeing with her. "She's going to be looking for allies. Abbie, do you think Palmer will come through and help us? I called around about him, and he's no small fish. He's got money, numbers and power."

"I don't think so. I haven't heard from him since we met at the café," I say, looking back to Skylar. "How fucking lucky are we? You have a mother who is psychotic and whose sole purpose in life is to kill the people you love. My mother is a liar who hid my father from me, and my father is the biggest drug dealer in Southern

California, who refuses to help me when I ask. We hit the parental jackpot."

"Exactly," Skylar replies. "When you put it that way, fuck."

Fuck indeed.

It takes a few hours to get back to the city, which we make use of, singing along to songs and stopping for snacks. I can't remember the last time I went on any kind of road trip with friends. The way here doesn't count because I was tied up, and it definitely didn't feel like I was with friends.

How things have changed.

We hear loud music coming from the clubhouse as soon as we park the car, and we all exchange glances.

"We're gone for one day and they're throwing a party?" I ask as I step out of the car.

"It seems that way," Skylar mutters, walking with me to the entrance, the men behind us. The music gets louder as we open the door and step inside, and when we hit the living room, the sight before us has my jaw dropping.

Dee is sitting there, in nothing but his black briefs, with a bottle of whiskey in his hand dragging along the floor, and getting a lap dance from some woman I've never seen before, also mostly naked.

"Well, that's more of Dee than I ever wanted to see," I admit, glancing away from his crotch area.

Dee finally notices us, and instead of being embarrassed in the slightest, he simply grins and mouths along to the Cardi B song that's playing. We leave him to his party and head out the back, where we find Chains and

Crow, both sitting there with their heads together looking at something.

"No women for you both?" Skylar asks, pulling out a chair next to Crow.

"Someone has to be responsible," Crow replies, lifting his head. "You know, just in case some mercenaries drop by. How did the trip to the country go?"

We give them the heads-up on Georgia.

"Great, for all we know she's walking around in disguise or some shit," Chains adds, glancing back inside. "Did we take a proper look at that stripper?"

"I doubt she can transform her body into a twenty-year-old's," Skylar replies in a dry tone. "She's not a witch. Well, I mean she is, but not in the magical sense."

"Call Renny," Temper says to Saint. "Let's head out. Crow, you come with me. Chains, you stay with Dee and the women."

"Wait, where are you going?" I ask, following him back inside.

"Going to go stake out the last place we saw Georgia. We thought we knew her home base back at the farm, but now we don't, and we need to get a step up on her. Need to find out where she's living, who she's surrounding herself with. I don't want to just sit around waiting for these men to try to jump us again, I'm not fuckin' having it." He lifts his T-shirt up and slides a gun into his jeans.

Shit.

"Okay, well, stay safe, all right?" I say, brow furrowing, eying the gun with worry. "Just remember, you have people here who love you and don't want anything to happen to you."

"Are those people you?" he asks, bending down to

give me a quick kiss. "Because I love you too, Abbie, and don't worry, I'll be fine. I'll be back later tonight, probably."

"Okay," I say softly.

Renny arrives with Izzy, and the men other than Chains and Dee head out on their mission, while we're stuck at home.

Again.

"So what do I need to be able to do to go out in the action, instead of be left home like a liability?" I ask Skylar, who laughs in return.

"Not be a liability?" she suggests, smirking. "The problem is that if we are there they are going to worry about us, and it's going to put them off their game. It has nothing to do with them not thinking we aren't capable enough. If we're here right now it's because they do think we can handle this life. You want to go spend some time in the gym? I can teach you a few more moves."

"Sounds good," I reply, needing the distraction. It's nice that she said that, because I don't want Temper thinking I'm some helpless damsel in distress, even though I know that I'm not as capable as them in these kind of situations.

I could be, though, one day.

And I will.

Chapter Twenty-Four

"Hello?" Skylar says into the phone. We both just did a workout, Izzy joining us toward the end, and now we're all dying on the floor, the soft mat underneath us cushioning our bodies.

"Who is this?" she asks, sitting up. "Mom?"

We're suddenly all on alert, and Izzy rushes off to call Chains in, the two of them returning in seconds.

"What do you mean you're in trouble? You're usually the one starting the trouble," Skylar states.

"Don't let on that we know she's involved," Chains whispers.

"Neville might have told her we went there, though, which would give it away," I also whisper.

Fuck, Izzy mouths. "Just see what she wants, but don't give anything away."

"I can't hear what you're saying, you're breaking up," Skylar says, frowning. "You want me to come and see you? You're hurt? Mom, I haven't even spoken to you in a very long time. Why are you calling me all of a sudden? Did you call Logan?"

She looks to us and covers the phone. "She's saying she's hurt and at the hospital, and wants me to come there to see her. She has something to tell me."

Chains shakes his head. "Ask her which hospital she's at and tell her you will be there soon."

Skylar asks, and recites the information out loud so we can all hear it.

"Okay, bye," she says, and hangs up the phone. "Oh my God, what is she planning now? She's probably going to try to kidnap me or something."

Chains is already on the phone to Temper, relaying what just happened. "What do you want us to do?" He nods a few times, and then hangs up the phone.

"What did he say?" I ask.

"He said to stay here, and they will head to the hospital. She's anticipating our next move, and she has to already know that we won't send Skylar in," he says, looking to the woman in question. "So what is she playing at then?"

"Maybe she wanted to draw the men out," I say, and we all share a look.

Chains instantly stands and rushes out the gym, probably going to check the security and put the clubhouse into lockdown mode.

"Let's go tell Dee what's going on," Izzy says, pulling me and Skylar up.

When we head to the living room however, there's no Dee. Izzy turns the music off, and calls out his name. "Dee?"

He's not where he was last seen, getting the dance from the stripper, and he's not in his bedroom, which is empty. We rush around the clubhouse looking for him, but he's nowhere to be seen.

"What the hell is going on?" I mutter to myself, sharing a look with Skylar. "Where could he have gone? He was drunk."

"I don't know. Let's keep looking, though," she says, and we split up, her going out the back and me going to the living room and kitchen once more.

"Dee's gone," I say to Chains when I run into him. "We've looked everywhere."

"The front gate was left open," he says to me, and then curses loudly. "Fuckin' hell. Come on, let's check the cameras."

I don't know why we didn't think of that from the start.

We all watch the security footage, and lo and behold, there's the fucking stripper dragging a passed-out Dee into his car and then driving away. I don't know how we let this happen, under all of our noses, but it has. I honestly didn't see this one coming, though. I need to start being suspicious of everything and everyone coming and going, because apparently you truly never know what the hell is going to happen next.

"You call Temper," Izzy whispers to me. "You're the only one of us who is not going to get murdered over this. Feel free to offer him sexual favors or something, anything, because he is going to lose his fucking shit."

"What do I say? 'Oh hey, Temper, we lost Dee. Yeah, I know there's four of us in here, but apparently we didn't even notice a stripper kidnapping him'?" I ask, eyes wide.

"Yes," Skylar replies, shrugging.

Fuck.

He answers on the first ring. "We have a huge problem," I say.

"What is it?" he asks, concern and worry laced in his tone. "Are you okay?"

"I'm okay," I promise. "But we don't know if Dee

is. The stripper kidnapped him—we just saw it on the camera. She must have drugged him, or maybe he was that drunk, I'm not sure, but she literally dragged his body into the car. She must do CrossFit or something, I don't know."

He's silent for a few seconds. "I'm sorry, what?"

"Tell us what we should do," I say to him.

"Put Chains on the phone," he growls.

"It's not Chains's fault, Temper, we were all—"

"Abbie, put him on. Now," he demands, tone full of steel.

Shit.

"Okay," I gulp, and hand Chains the phone.

We can all hear the yelling through the phone, and I feel so bad. I've never heard Temper use that tone before, and it's fucking scary. He sounds so mean, and he's obviously lost control of his temper. I'm finally seeing how he got his name.

If he ever spoke to me like that, I'd probably cry.

No, I would definitely cry.

I don't know how all four of us let a stranger one-up us, but it happened, and it's not a good feeling, especially after the chat I just had with Skylar about not wanting to be a damn liability. I know it's none of our faults, but we could have paid a little more attention and checked in on Dee, who we knew was drunk and acting a fool.

Chains ends the call and scrubs his hand down his face. "What a fuckin' mess. Temper's coming back here now, Saint and Renny are staying there and seeing what's going down at the hospital. Heaven help us all."

"He's not that mad, right? I mean, he got the yelling over and done with, so I'm sure he's going to walk back into the clubhouse with a clear head and an idea to fix this whole mess."

Chains gives me a funny look, then pats the top of my head. "Ahhh, Abbie. Love truly is blind."

We watch him walk away, looking like he's about to go to a funeral.

"What's going to happen now?" I ask the girls.

"We're going to have to go and find Dee or wait until the stripper calls us and tells us what she wants," Skylar guesses, covering her face with her hands. "What the fuck else can go wrong today? I don't even know what's happening anymore. I need a drink."

"No one is drinking, you've seen what happens," Izzy murmurs, leading us back into the living room. "I can't believe this has happened. I mean, everyone should have questioned why Dee had a stripper in the clubhouse, but it's not like the men haven't done this kind of shit. Mainly before we came into the picture, but still."

"I don't think anyone saw this coming." Skylar sighs, glancing down at her phone. "I didn't see my mom calling me either, though, so let's just say that anything is possible right now. I messaged my brother Logan asking him if Mom called, and he said no. So it must be bullshit, because Logan is her firstborn and favorite; there's no way she wouldn't have called him if something was truly wrong."

"Maybe she was distracting us so the stripper could sneak Dee out," I suggest, wincing. "I mean, it did the trick."

Skylar blinks slowly a few times. "Fuck."

"What does she want with Dee, though?" I ask.

"Maybe he was the only one she could get a hold of. I

mean, he's been going to that strip club a while now. Remember, he even wanted some new clothes to impress some chick. Maybe Georgia noticed that and got the girl on her side," Izzy suggests, tapping her long nail on her cheek. "I just don't see where she's going to take it from here. There's nothing in particular that she wants, right? What the hell is she going to do with Dee?"

"Use him to make us do what she wants?" I guess. "Who knows? I guess we're going to find out, but I hope Dee is okay."

"Temper will find him," Skylar says with conviction. She believes in her president, there's no doubt.

We hear Temper before we see him. "You had four people to protect," he says to Chains, his sinister voice echoing through the clubhouse. "I trusted you, and now Dee is fuckin' gone. I am seething, Chains. Seething."

"I know I fucked up," Chains admits. "I'm sorry. I'll do anything to get him back, all right? Just tell me what you need me to do."

Crow comes over to us and sits down on the couch. "This is fucked."

"So fucked," Izzy adds, touching Crow's shoulder. "What the hell are we going to do now?"

"I'm going to stay with you. Temper and Chains are going to try to get Dee back," he explains to us.

"How are they going to do that?" I ask them.

"They're going to the strip club Dee has been going to recently and go from there. I don't know if there is a concrete plan—I think they're just going to have to wing it."

That sounds fucking stressful.

"I'm going to go and change the code on the gate, because we don't know if the stripper knows it. Dee was out of it. Fuck it, I'm changing the codes on everything. You three, do not fucking separate, and do not move. I'm not allowing anything else to go wrong today."

"Okay," we all say at the same time.

"I've never heard Crow speak like that to us," Skylar points out. "He must be freaking out."

Temper enters the room, his eyes coming right to me. I get up and go to him without a word, and his arms come around me. "It could be worse, at least that's what I'm telling myself."

"They aren't going to hurt Dee, are they?" I ask softly, brow furrowing. "I just don't understand how we are going to fix this."

We.

I'm as invested in this as they are.

"You just worry about staying safe, all right? I'll go and get Dee back, only so I can kick his ass myself," he mutters, resting his forehead against mine. "Please, stay here and stay out of fuckin' trouble. I love you."

"We will, and I love you too," I promise him. "Stay safe. If Georgia is involved, I think we can agree we don't know what to expect."

"And next time one of the men try to use you like a fuckin' shield for my anger, tell them to fuck off," he growls, kisses me, and then leaves the room.

"Dee is going to be all right, isn't he?" I ask them, cuddling in between them on the couch, watching the door Temper just left through.

So much can go wrong right now, and it's nerve wracking just waiting here and hoping for the best.

"Yep, he will be fine," Skylar says. "We will all be fine."

She sounds confident, but I'm not so sure.

They have no real plan. We don't know what they want with Dee in the first place, or what they have up their sleeve, and we have no idea what they're about to walk into. I can almost feel my mom's anxiety flowing through me, or is that my own now?

"Is Ariel going to be okay?" Skylar asks Izzy. "Are they alone at your house?"

"No, they're all at Trade's house, so they will be fine," Izzy replies, frowning. "But I left Shadow at home—I should have brought him here. He would have barked anytime anyone came near the clubhouse."

Crow comes in, and hands us each a loaded gun. "You all know what to do?"

We all nod, and I'm so glad I took the time to learn how to shoot and use various guns, or I'd be so fucked right now.

"Okay, good. Just a precaution," he says, eying each of us in turn. "We don't know what to expect right now, but we've got this. No one is going to come here and try to fuck with us, I'm going to make sure of that."

Crow has clearly been pushed to his breaking point, and fair enough—they fucked with one of us.

And now they can pay the price.

Chapter Twenty-Five

When we hear someone yelling at the front of the club-house, we all share a look.

"What the hell is going on now?" I whisper, looking to Crow. "What do we do?"

"Temper knows the new code," he says, frowning. "Come on, stay behind me."

We all go to the front of the clubhouse, guns in hand, and peer through the window. Standing there is Chains, and he's carrying Dee in his arms.

"Open the gate," Skylar says quickly. "It's Chains and Dee!"

Crow rushes out and lets them in. If he only told Temper the new code, I guess the other two wouldn't know it, but where is Temper? I look behind them, waiting for him to arrive. Did they go in two cars? Or did he take his bike?

Chains comes inside, carrying a battered Dee, who is sporting a broken nose and is covered in blood. "Is he okay?" Izzy asks Chains, touching Dee's face.

My heart is racing, and I don't know if it's because Dee looks like he's been through hell, or because Temper has still yet to walk through those doors to tell me that everything is going to be okay.

"He's fine, just a little beaten up," Chains says.

"Where's Temper?" I ask him, brow furrowing. "Why isn't he with you?"

What happened out there?

Chains ignores me, and continues to carry Dee into his bedroom, laying him on top of the sheets. I follow behind, waiting for someone to tell me what the hell is going on and where my man is. I can feel myself about to snap, about to lose control as panic and fear start to take over me. Skylar looks over Dee, and tells us that he's a little battered, but going to be okay.

"Chains," Crow says, stopping him with his arm on his shoulder. "What happened?"

"We went into the stripper's bar—they were expecting us. All the mercenaries were there, about ten of them, not to mention Georgia, and there was more of them than there was us. They offered Temper a trade. Him for Dee, and we get to walk away unharmed. If he didn't agree to that trade, they were going to kill us all, starting with Dee."

"I can't believe Georgia. I think I'm going to be sick," Skylar says, running to the bathroom.

"Fuck," Crow whispers, turning to me, and pulling me against him. "Abbie, it's going to be okay. We'll get him back. He's not going out like this, no way in hell."

I'm still trying to process the whole thing. So now we have Dee back, but they have Temper? Was this their plan all along? What are they going to do to him? Does he look like Dee does right now? Are they hurting him? What if Georgia has had enough playing around and is going to kill him? What if he's already gone?

He said he'd come home to me.

I guess being with the president means being with someone who will always put himself last, someone who always has to be the hero. But you know what?

Crow is right: Temper is not going out like this.

"Where is this stripper's bar?" I demand from Chains. "Where?" I yell when he doesn't reply. "Tell me!"

I don't care what I have to do, but I'm going to try anything.

I did not just get this man only to lose him.

"What are you going to do?" Skylar asks me as she comes back from the bathroom, holding on to my arm and making me look at her. "You can't just walk in there, Abbie. Temper would be devastated if you did that, and it wouldn't end well. The men just tried the same thing and look at what happened. We need a new plan, a better plan, or this isn't going to end well."

"*I'm* devastated!" I growl. "I don't care what Temper thinks right now, I just want to save him. He might not be around to care if we don't do something now. And I don't care what I have to do. You're right, I just need a better plan."

Think, Abbie, think.

"Georgia was there?" I ask Chains.

He nods. "Yeah, she was. The mercenaries are hers. She's calling the shots."

Shit.

"I've got an idea," I say, looking at each of them in turn. "But I'm going to need all of you, and Skylar, I'm going to need a huge fucking favor from you."

"Anything you need," she instantly says.

I don't know if this is going to work, but I'm sure as hell going to try anything that I can.

"Skylar, I can't be fucking walking into some situation where I'm going to get shot. I have a family and I need to be there for them," Logan says, shaking his head.

"We have a family too," she says. "And it's our

mother pulling this bullshit, and you're her favorite kid. You're the only leverage we have over her."

"Please," I say, looking him dead in the eye. "I can't lose him."

Logan groans, his head falling back on his neck. "I cannot believe you are trying to drag me into this shit. Are you sure Mom is the ringleader of this? I don't know what the hell is going on, Skylar."

"Logan, you don't know me." I start willing him to understand the severity of the situation. "But your mother has hired men to come after the MC. And while that may not affect you, I get it, but on both those occasions innocent people were around and could've been hurt. The first time, I was there and could've been shot. The second time your sister, Izzy and myself were also there. She doesn't care who gets hurt as long as she gets her revenge, and that even means Skylar. Your mother is a loose cannon."

Logan looks back and forth between me and Skylar, and I think he must sense my desperation. "All right, come on."

I don't know how the hell we talked him into this, but it was all I could think of, because I remember Skylar telling me how Logan was Georgia's favorite and that she really did love him. It's all I can think to use against her, but I know it's a long shot. It's not often people will agree to walk into a strip club and face a potential gun fight, pretending to be a captor we will harm if she doesn't do a trade.

Temper for Logan.

I just pray that this is going to work.

We take two separate cars, Skylar, Saint and Logan driving together, and me with Renny, Crow, Chains and

Izzy. We left Dee with Trade and Ariel, so they can look after him and make sure that he's going to be all right.

We're basically on a damn suicide mission right now, and I don't know how this is going to end, but if any of these people get hurt, I'm not sure how I'm going to live with myself. If anything happens to Temper, though, I would be fucked. Is this the shit they have to deal with all the time? The decisions they have to make? How do they do it?

"Tell me that we're doing the right thing," I say out loud.

"We're doing the best we can, and that's all we can do," Renny assures me, looking over at me from the corner of his eye. "Knights don't give up and don't back down. We're doing the right thing. We're fighting for us."

"Okay." I feel selfish bringing Logan into this, and I'm just hoping that it all goes to plan.

It has to go to plan.

"There's the place," Renny says, looking toward a run-down bar on the corner of an old street.

"This is Dee's hangout?" Izzy asks, judgment in her tone. "Hasn't he heard of Toxic? He should go there— that strip club is fire."

"Dee met that girl online," Crow explains. "After they had a date and she told him where she worked, this place became his hangout."

"He has the worst taste in women," Izzy grumbles.

"Last time we went in the back way," Renny explains. "I doubt they're expecting us back today, after how it went down the first time. I'm not sure if they will still have Temper there, or if they've moved him. We're going in blind, guys. Let's hope for the best but prepare for the worst."

"How will they contain him?" I ask. "He's a big man, and he's not going to take this lying down, especially after you all got out safely."

"I don't know," Renny admits. "Maybe they've drugged him. They have numbers, and weapons. He's big, but he's not invincible."

"Okay, so what's the plan? You already stormed in through the back, but we can't just waltz in through the front, either. They'd recognize us straight away," I say, pursing my lips. "Well, they might not recognize me. Would they? Am I on Georgia's radar?" Renny and I share a look. "Are you thinking what I'm thinking?"

"That Temper is going to fuckin' murder me with his bare hands if we let you go in as bait?" Renny replies, lips tightening. "How the hell are you going to ask me to send you in as bait right now, Abbie? There has to be another way. If something goes wrong, I don't need more blood on my hands."

"He has to be alive for him to murder you," I point out, arching my brow. "I'm the only face they won't recognize on sight. I'm the best option that we have, Renny. Admit it. They're not going to expect some random girl the MC just met to come in, guns blazing. They'd expect me to be sitting at home hoping that one of you with a penis saves the day."

I mean, there's a chance the mercenaries will recognize me from the club, but they might not even be there. We have no other plan, and if I can help in some way, even if it's just a little bit, I'm going to damn well do it.

"He's going to kill us," Renny says, looking behind at the rest of the crew. "You're all aware of this, right. He's going to go Hulk Smash and destroy us."

"Yeah, but we have to get him out of there first," Izzy

says. "So Abbie, you go in, pretend to be a customer, see what's going on, create a diversion or something so we can break in through the back and try to save his ass?"

"You're not going in," Renny tells her, scowling.

"The hell I'm not," Izzy replies.

"Someone has to stay in the car and be ready to drive away the escape vehicle," he says.

"This is the worst plan ever," I tell them all. "But fuck it, let's do it. Let's wing it. And let's hope Saint and the others get the memo."

We got here before them, but they should be arriving any second now.

"I feel like this is something we should definitely not wing," Chains deadpans. "I'll call Saint and tell him the plan, or lack thereof."

"We have no other choice, we are fucking winging it," I grumble.

Renny parks down the road from the strip club, and I get out first, and take a deep breath.

Fuck.

Let's go see some strippers.

Chapter Twenty-Six

"You want a drink?" one of the girls at the bar asks me.

"Sure," I reply, forcing a smile. "A margarita, please."

"Ohhh, you're fancy," she replies, making it sound like that's a bad thing. I don't know when ordering a cocktail became fancy, but as I take in the run-down bar, and the women who work here, I can tell that maybe they aren't really cocktail type of people.

"I try," I reply, staring at the woman dancing on stage, my eyes then darting to the hall. I don't know how I'm going to pull this off, but I'm going to have to try something.

She slides me my drink and I place some money on the table. "You know if this place is hiring?" I ask, thinking that it might be a good angle to use.

"Actually, we are," she says, eying me from face to breasts and back up again. "And you know what, we have women of all shapes and sizes now."

I don't know if that was a dig or a compliment, but I'm going to go with the former. "Really? Well, isn't that lucky for a woman who looks like me," I reply in a dry tone and a fake smile. "How does one audition? Do you have a manager or someone I could speak to about it?"

I didn't think this is how our conversation was going to go, but whatever works.

"My manager is out back, but I could go find her for you. We need some fresh meat around here. I think the customers are getting bored," she admits in a low tone, rolling her blue eyes.

"Oh no, we can't have that. I guess new faces might bring in some extra tips, hey?"

Her eyes light up. "Exactly, I'll be right back."

She disappears into the back, and after a few seconds, I follow her, walking down a hallway with various rooms. I hear her voice talking to another woman, and duck down, stopping at one of the last rooms when I hear a man's voice.

"He's unconscious still," one of the men says. "What does she want us to do with him?"

"Take him to her house," another man replies. "And then our job is done, and we get our money. I'm never accepting another contract from her again. Our enemy list is growing just being associated with her."

"I know, me neither. But it wasn't too hard of a job, you have to admit. We didn't even have to kill him."

"I know, I think she's going to do that herself."

A pause, and then, "If she was younger and not as crazy, I'd marry her."

Laughter.

Georgia wants to kill Temper herself? The bitch truly is psychotic.

Abbie: He's here, in the very back room. Unconscious. Men around him.

Renny: GET OUT OF THERE NOW.

I don't.

Instead, I sneak in the room opposite the one Temper is in, and crouch down low in the darkness. I don't know where Georgia is, but frankly I'd rather take on the hired killers than her. Touching the gun tucked into my jeans, I know I'm either going to have to make my next move, or get the hell out of here. I just don't know which. I know it sounds stupid, but I don't want to leave Temper. He's in the next room, and I don't want to walk out of here unless he's going to be with me.

If I left and we weren't able to save him, I'd never forgive myself.

"I want him taken to this address," a woman says. "And then you will get your payment. Make sure he is secure, for when the drugs wear off. I don't want him to be able to get away."

"Yes, ma'am," the man replies.

"Good, I will meet you there in an hour."

Without thinking, I step toward her voice, pulling out my gun and pointing it in the direction of the door opposite me.

I have no idea what I'm doing, and I'm scared shitless, but this bitch needs to be taken down a notch. I'm sick of her. And I'm sick of her targeting Temper, who has done nothing to her.

"Well, what do we have here?" She laughs, her shrewd green eyes on the weapon in my hands. "Abbie, isn't it? My ace in the hole. You were a pleasant surprise. Foolish girl, there are five men here with guns, guns that are bigger, badder and more well used than yours. I really don't want to see you hurt, so why don't you walk back out and return to your small town? Did you think you were just going to leave here with the president? He's mine."

That's where she is wrong.

"You're a little too old for him, Granny," I reply, stepping closer to her, clicking the safety off and aiming right at her face. I can feel the presence of the men, her minions, but no one makes a move. "What have you done to him? If you've hurt him…"

"Oh, nothing yet," she says, flashing her teeth. "You know I used to be where you are right now. I'd caught the eye of the president of the Knights. I was well respected. I was living my best life. It all comes to an end, though, and it's not worth losing your life over. So why don't you walk away, while you still have the chance?"

"Temper did nothing to you," I state. "And Hammer is gone, you made sure of that."

"You don't know Temper," she replies, eyes narrowing. "He is not a good man. Yet you'll stand by him? I thought you'd be smarter than that. All of the Knights. They poisoned my daughter against me. They tainted my Hammer against me. Temper especially. Hammer would be alive and none of this would've happened if Temper had just minded his own business!" She screams the last part.

The two men step out behind her, guns pointed right at me.

"He's good to me."

"And to us," Saint says from behind me, Logan in front of him, gun at his temple. "Give us Temper, or your golden child gets it."

"Logan?" Georgia whispers, eyes flickering. "You wouldn't hurt him. Skylar wouldn't forgive you."

"Skylar doesn't have to know." Saint smiles evilly.

"And who would she believe, you or me? Besides, Temper is the man she sees as her new father figure. She happens to have a shitload of brothers too, so I'm sure she could survive losing one."

"Mom?" Logan says, swallowing hard. "What the hell is going on here? Why are you doing this?"

"Logan, I'm sorry," she says. "I don't know why they're bringing you into this."

"Just give them what they want, please, Mom," he says, eyes pleading. "I'm too young to die." At this point, I don't know if Logan is just playing the part or really thinks he's about to die from a bullet, but I have no idea how this is going to play out either.

Saint's finger lingers on the trigger. "I'm not fucking around, Georgia. What do you love more? Your son or revenge?"

She eyes her firstborn. "Okay, fine. Give them Temper," she says to the men behind her. "Now!"

The men drag him out, and he's still out cold, his body limp.

"My men are waiting at the back door. Gently carry him to them, and they will take him. Only then is Logan safe," Saint demands, clearly much better at this whole thing. "If anyone tries anything, your firstborn is going to be the first in the ground."

"You heard him," Georgia commands her men. "Do as he says."

The men carry Temper out, where Renny and everyone else are waiting, guns pointed. Chains puts down his gun to carry Temper into the car, while the other men keep their guns ready to go, in case someone doesn't stick to their word.

"Now give me Logan and leave," she demands.

"Not so fast," Saint replies, flashing me a look that he clearly wants me to read, but I can't. What does he want me to do? Does he want me to shoot one of the men? I mean, I guess I could shoot someone in the foot or something. It wouldn't kill them, just hurt them a lot.

Temper is now safely outside, but what about Georgia? If we just leave her here, she's just going to come back for us again.

Maybe he wants me to shoot *her*?

We're still having this silent one-sided conversation and I have no idea what's going on. If it was Temper trying to tell me something, I'd probably be able to understand, but I don't speak Saint, and I'm about to freak the fuck out.

"Let Logan go," Georgia says, and Saint moves the gun from Logan to her. Logan walks over to his mom, not standing too close, probably just in case someone decides to take the evil bitch out.

Four men return, and now all of a sudden we are fucked again, because we have two guns against their four. I'm pretty sure this was the situation Saint was trying to get us out of, but I didn't understand what he wanted me to do, and I froze. Now I'm fucked.

"Put your guns down, or she dies," Saint tells them.

They eye her, and she nods, telling them to lower their weapons. They all do so at the same time, but they're on alert, watching and waiting for their moment. This isn't going to end well, and I know that. I don't see how we're just going to be able to walk out of here.

"Mom, enough," Logan demands. "Come on, let's get out of here. I don't feel well. I don't understand why you'd want to hurt the MC you know your daughter is a part of, and one where you used to be queen bee. It doesn't make any sense."

Logan, the hero we didn't know we needed but got anyway.

"You don't understand," she says to him, shaking her head. "The MC betrayed me, and now they deserve all they get. I gave my life to them, and look how they repaid me. First they took Hammer, and then they took Skylar from me," she wails. "I was the strong female leader the MC needed. I should be in charge, not her." She points to me.

Okay, now I'm getting angry. "It's not up to you; that decision is up to Temper. You have nothing to do with the Knights anymore, aside from the fact that your daughter is well loved by them. You're a has-been."

Her face contorts in anger.

Oops.

Saint throws me a look that clearly says *shut the fuck up*, but how dare she? This old woman is holding on to the past, on to something that doesn't even exist anymore. She's not a Knight. She knows nothing about loyalty, about family. She doesn't even love her own daughter like a mother is supposed to.

"You know nothing. The club will chew you up and spit you out just like they did me." She sneers.

The back door flies open again, but this time I have to do a double take at who I see standing there.

"What are you doing here?" I ask my father, frowning. Does he have something to do with this?

Grayson is standing there in a three-piece pinstripe suit. He looks strong and powerful. This is the kingpin I've heard about, amber eyes that match my own jumping between me and Georgia. "Get the fuck out of here if you ever want to work in this city again," he says in a deathly tone to the hitmen.

It was like all the air got sucked out of the room. The four men immediately start filing out of the room, almost tripping over one another.

"You signed a contract!" Georgia screams at them as they leave. "And you work for me until that contract is done! Don't you dare listen to him."

When she realizes they aren't going to come back, she turns her lunacy on Saint. "What are you going to do? You can't hurt me. My daughter is the love of your life, so I'm untouchable. None of you would ever so much as lay a finger on me, especially in front of my son, which means I will win every fucking time. I don't care which of you die, but none of you have the balls to do anything to me. Skylar won't allow it—"

I aim at her foot and pull the trigger. I don't know what comes over me, whether it was her speech or the fact that she almost had the man I love killed, but I'm done with her shit.

"Skylar might be the love of Saint's life, but she's not mine. Temper is, and you chose to fuck with him," I say, as she gasps, blood pouring on the floor.

"Oh my God!" she cries out, trying to stop the bleeding with her hands. "Help me!"

Logan takes off his jacket and helps his mom stop the bleeding, knowing that while it's probably very painful, she won't die from it. He probably doesn't like me much right now, but I owe him a solid, because he really helped us here today.

He turns to Grayson. "Neville, what are you doing here? How are you involved with this? I thought you and my mom split up."

Neville?

Wait, Grayson is *Neville*? The farmer husband?

Hold the fucking phone. How many fucking aliases does this man have?

"You went after my daughter," he says to Georgia, tone cold and emotionless. "That's where you fucked up. And now you've lost everything. The second you sent those mercenaries near Abbie, you fucked up your life. I kicked you out of the house because I was done with you, but never did I think you'd be so stupid to go after her twice."

"I didn't know she was your daughter then!" Georgia defends herself, crying. "How was I supposed to know? You didn't even know! And she walked into this bar; I didn't go after her. She came after me."

Which is actually true, but she had something that belonged to me.

I look at Grayson, who turns his back on Georgia and comes straight to me. I have so many questions that want to come out, but he speaks first. "There will be a time for explanation, but not today. Get out of here, Abbie. I'll take care of everything, okay?"

I have so many questions right now, I don't even know where to start.

Saint grabs for my arm, taking the gun from my hand. "Come on, let's get out of here. Let's process this Neville thing later, because I'm as fucking confused as you are."

Leaving Georgia bleeding on the floor but very much alive, with her son and her husband—my dad—by her side, we make our escape.

There is silence until I can't stand it anymore. "Hey,

Saint. What were you trying to tell me with your eyes before my father walked in?"

Saint laughed. "I was trying to tell you to get the hell out of there. But there you were packing heat and ready to shoot at will." He looks at me with a bit of awe. "I can't believe you shot her. Who the fuck are you?"

"Temper's old lady. I protect what's mine." I get into the back seat with Temper, who is still very much unconscious, and we drive home. He comes to just as we pull into the clubhouse, as if he sensed that we were home.

"Hey," I say, smiling and touching his cheek. "You're awake."

He smiles sleepily, then winces and rubs the back of his head. "What happened? Georgia—"

"It's okay, you're safe now. We're all safe," I assure him.

I kiss his forehead.

I shot a woman in the foot today, and for this man, I'd do it all over again.

Chapter Twenty-Seven

"I heard that you shot my mom," Skylar says the next day, coming to sit next to me on my bed.

"Yeah, sorry about that. She just really triggered me," I admit, frowning. "She was going on about how she will always win because she's untouchable because of you."

And I mean, she walked away again, so maybe it's true.

Or at least this time, she limped away.

"Don't be sorry," she says. "She deserved it. In fact she got off lightly and we all know that. I'd never be able to do anything to her—at the end of the day, she's still my mom—but after all she's done I could never hold a grudge against anyone who…"

She trails off, unable to finish the sentence. "I understand."

She shrugs. "And my stepdad is your real father. Does that make us related?"

"Yeah, I don't think any of us saw that one coming."

She wraps her arm around me. "Neville, I mean Grayson, is a really nice man. He's always been nothing but kind to me, so maybe don't write him off right away. He deserves a fucking Oscar nomination for playing the nice little old farmer, though. I tell you what, I never once thought he would be capable of doing anything illegal."

I rub my forehead. "I don't even know what to think about Grayson. I think you're right, he's good at playing whatever part he needs to, which makes him a little hard to trust. He did have my back, though, and I'm not going to forget that."

"Blood ties are strong," she agrees. "I'm just glad Temper is back and everyone is safe. I don't know how we managed to pull that off. Izzy and I got stuck playing getaway driver, while the new girl got in on all the action."

I laugh at that. "I was so scared, I'm not going to lie. I had no idea what I was doing, or what was going to happen. Tell Logan I said thank you, though, and I'm sorry for shooting his mom and then leaving him to deal with it."

Her lip twitches. "Yeah, I'm sure I'm going to hear a rant from him, but it was worth it. We all did what we had to. We are a great team."

"We are," I admit, my smile fading. "And as soon as Temper is feeling better, it's time for me to go home."

"I don't want you to go," she confesses. "You belong here, with us."

"I'll be back," I promise, because I agree, I do. "I just need to tie up all my loose ends over there, and make sure my mom and sister will be okay without me there to help out."

"Well, if you need any extra help, give us a call, and we'll be there," she says, lifting her face as Temper exits the bathroom, towel wrapped around him. "Okay, I'm out. Nice to see you up and well, Prez."

He gives her a warm smile, and watches her leave. "I feel much better now."

"Good." On top of knocking him out with a hit to the head, we think they gave him something to make sure he'd stay unconscious for a longer period of time, leaving him groggy.

"Saint gave me a rundown of the whole retrieval mission," he says, sitting down on the bed. "I can't believe you did all of that for me. Do you know the amount of danger you put yourself in?"

"Yes, but it all paid off. I wasn't going to let them just take you and do nothing. I might not be as badass as you all, but I'd do anything to protect the people that I love," I say, shuffling closer to him and resting my head on his shoulder. "You would have done the same for me, or for anyone else in the MC."

"What do you mean you're not as badass?" He chuckles, kissing the top of my head. "From what I've heard, you're the most badass out of us all. You led a team, made executive decisions, shot Georgia... You sure you're not here to steal my job?"

"No, just your heart." I grin.

He pushes me back on the bed and looks me dead in the eye. "I'm not happy you put yourself in danger. I'm not happy my men allowed you to do so. But I'm happy to be here, with you, and you've made me really fuckin' proud. You're a woman everyone here could look up to, and you've proven that you're right where you're meant to be."

"Yeah, they thought you were going to kill them," I say. "Please don't blame them. I went in guns blazing."

"So I've heard. And Neville being Grayson. How do you feel about that?"

"I don't know," I admit. "I need to speak to him before I leave. It's a lot to process."

He throws his towel on the floor, and we slide under the sheets and cuddle.

"And if you're going to give yourself up to save the others, it's only fair that I'm allowed to do whatever I need to do to save you," I say, yawning. "Sometimes the hero needs to be saved, too. You can't be everything for everyone, without someone at your back, looking out for you. Your cup needs to be filled before you can pour it out for others."

He rubs his fingers up and down my arm, goose bumps appearing on my flesh. "My cup will always be filled with you around. I don't know how the fuck I'm supposed to leave you and come back here alone."

"We'll be fine," I assure him. "It won't be for too long, anyway."

A connection like this can last through anything, there's no doubt in my mind.

Moving on top of him, straddling his body, I kiss him, then sit up and smile down at him. "I love you."

"I love you," he replies, watching me with hooded eyes as I pull off my T-shirt and bra, leaving me in just a pair of leggings. From this angle he can see my stomach, my breasts, close up, all of my imperfections. But he still looks at me like I'm the most beautiful woman he's ever seen.

And to him, I am.

I don't regret waiting for someone who makes me feel like this.

Taking a chance on Temper is the best thing I ever did.

"I'm sure you both have a lot of questions," Grayson says the next day, glancing between me and Skylar.

When he finally reached out, he asked that both Skylar and I come to meet him together. We chose to meet at a restaurant.

"You can say that again," Skylar says, studying him in a new light. "I knew you as this gentle, modest farmer, one I didn't think knew my mother was an evil witch, yet you're some kingpin who has probably never farmed a day in his life."

He chuckles under his breath. "I grew up on that farm. It's been in my family for generations. And I do maintain it, so you're wrong there. Technically, I am also a farmer. And Abbie, one day that farm will be yours."

"It's so weird, Skylar knowing you more than me," I admit. "I mean, she knew you as a different person under a different name, but still."

He studies me for a few seconds. "I met Georgia after she was kicked out of the Knights. Despite what you think, Skylar, your mother was very honest with me about who she was and I was honest with her on who I was. I was with Georgia for years, and yes, the whole gentle farmer thing was a front, one she agreed to play into."

"You always seemed to love her. Worship her even…" Skylar says, confusion in her voice.

"I don't know what to say right now," I murmur, my eyes scanning his. "How could you be with a woman like that for so long?"

Grayson blushes a bit and coughs. "Abbie, good girls don't really often come my way doing what I do. And if one did, I probably wouldn't know what to do with her. Look what happened with your mom, for example. With your mother, we could've really had something, but when she found out what I did to earn a living, she ended things and told me she never wanted to see me again. I didn't know she was pregnant at the time, but she couldn't handle this life and I understood that. You might not see it, but I did love Georgia. She was the first woman with whom I didn't have to hide who I am. Georgia... Georgia loved me for me. She knew the score. So I treated her like a queen."

Skylar and I just sit there staring at him.

"You have amber eyes," Skylar blurts out. "I always thought they were brown. Do you wear contacts?"

Grayson nods. "I do. My eyes are very unique." He looks to me. "They are hard to forget, and in my line of work I can't be memorable."

"When did you find out what Georgia was up to?" I ask. "Did you know when we met at the café?"

"No, but after you mentioned your friend Skylar with a mother who hired mercenaries, I went home and confronted her. She admitted she hired mercenaries to kill Temper. She told me about what happened in your hometown, and the second I found out, I kicked her out of the house and wanted nothing else to do with her."

"Wait. When I came to see you, you acted like you had no idea and were really upset. But you knew then? Why didn't you just tell me?" Skylar asks, and I can see her clenching her fists.

"I'm sorry about that. I didn't know exactly what she was planning with the MC, and when you came I was in the middle of getting answers. So it was easier to pretend so I could get to the bottom of it and then explain everything. But when I found out what was going on with Temper, I—"

"Who are you?" Skylar asks, frowning. "I've known you as this one man for so many years and now you're sitting here someone completely different. How am I supposed to know which is true?"

"This." He gestures to himself. He's not in the three-piece suit this time, but he is in what I would call business casual. Slacks and a collared shirt. Kind of like a farmer at a business meeting. "This is who I am. I am a farmer who participates in other business activities. But the person I was with you, Skylar, was me." He looks to me. "And Abbie, I know you don't know me, but I'd like to change that."

"So do we call you Grayson, Neville, or Cohen?" I ask, changing the subject and lightening the mood. I don't know how I feel about the whole situation, but I want to at least give him a chance.

"Dad works," he says, glancing down shyly. "But otherwise Grayson."

I don't think I'm ready for Dad just yet, so Grayson it is.

"I just wanted to say I'm sorry," Dee says the next morning, as I'm packing my things to leave. "I fucked up, badly. I never should have brought Cherry back to the clubhouse. I never should have trusted her. My dick got us all in trouble, and I'm really sorry, Abbie. I hope you can forgive me."

I go up and give him a hug. He still looks so sore, rocking a black eye, broken nose and split lip, and I don't want to leave here with him feeling like shit, blaming himself for everything that happened.

"Of course I forgive you. You didn't know Cherry was going to drug and kidnap you," I say. "I mean, how could you? We didn't even think anything of it."

"You're the best, you know that?" he says. "I'm so glad Temper found someone like you."

"Thank you," I say, kissing him on the cheek.

"Okay, let's not get me further beat up," he grumbles, winking at me and leaving the room.

I finish up packing, and then drag my suitcase to the living room. "I'm ready when you are!" I call out to Temper. The clubhouse is quiet, and I wonder where the hell everyone is. I know I told them all that I'll be back soon, but only Dee came to say goodbye. Not even Skylar and Izzy have been here today.

Temper walks into the room and offers me his hand. "I guess we better get going then." He drags my suitcase with his free hand and leads me outside.

"We're going to miss you, Abbie!" the MC screams, where they're all waiting for me out front with a giant sign, balloons and the biggest of smiles.

I rush to the girls and hug them first, then each of the men in turn.

"I thought you guys had forgotten to come and say goodbye to me," I admit, rubbing my eyes. Some dust seems to have gotten in there.

"Are you kidding me?" Izzy says. "We're going to miss you so much!"

"Come back soon," Saint says, kissing the top of my head.

"I will," I promise.

Temper puts my suitcase in the car, his bag already packed and in there, and off we go. I wave until I lose sight of them. I wouldn't think it would be so hard to leave people I've only known for such a short time, but it is.

"They're all so wonderful," I say to Temper, turning the radio on.

"They love you," he says, pride in his tone.

"This is our first official road trip with just me and you," I say, reaching over and kissing his rough cheek. "Are you ready for this adventure?"

"Am I ready to face the wrath of your mom and sister is the question," he murmurs, turning his face to give me a quick kiss.

"You telling me that the big, bad president is scared of my mom?" I tease. "Don't worry about it, it will be fine. I'm sure she's not going to be thrilled about the situation, but it doesn't matter. I love you, and I know I want to be with you, and that's all that matters to me. Once they see how happy I am, I'm sure they will get on board."

"I hope so."

Truth be told, I hope so too.

"It will be fine. How long do you think you're going to stay for?" I ask. He said that he's going to stay at the hotel, the one he took me on our first date to, and that I'm welcome to stay there with him.

"Three nights," he says. "I've left Saint in charge, and hopefully nothing else goes wrong while I'm gone."

"I think we've had our share of bad luck this week," I say. "Hopefully its over for now. Or forever."

"One can hope. Georgia's foot will have bought us some time, but who knows what she's going to plan next?" he says, looking over at me. "We're going to have to come up with a solution soon enough."

"I know," I agree. "We all can't go on like this forever. And she's never going to stop, she's admitted as much. It's just such a shame for Skylar. I feel so bad for her."

"I know, we all do."

The first hour of the trip is spent singing along to the radio. It's not soon before I fall asleep, not being the best road trip partner. I'm woken by Temper yelling loudly, and I practically jump out of my seat.

"What is it? What?" I ask, glancing around in a panic.

Temper, the asshole, starts losing it laughing. He takes his phone from where he'd placed it on the dashboard, right in front of me, and replays the clip, one that is not flattering to me in any shape or form. "Look at your face." He laughs.

"You recorded that?" I ask, scowling. "I'm going to get you back, you know that, right?"

"Look how wide your eyes go," he continues, pushing my damn buttons.

I shove the phone away from me. "Why are we stopped here?"

"I'm hungry, thought we could stop and get something to eat. But you were fast asleep and snoring."

"So you decided to wake me up by screaming and scaring the shit out of me?" I ask, undoing my seat belt. I get out of the car and stretch my legs.

"Ah, come on, don't be like that," he says, wrapping his arms around me. "I'm just playing with you."

I stick my tongue out at him. "Come on and feed me then."

"You hangry, babe?" he teases, opening the door for me.

Rolling my eyes, I step inside, and then check out the menu.

Little does Temper know, he just started a prank war.

One he isn't going to win.

Chapter Twenty-Eight

As we start to get closer to home, my nerves kick in.
I know my mom isn't going to let me off lightly. She's
going to have a million questions, and she'll expect that
I answer them in detail. Some of the answers I know
I'm not going to have…or at least I'm not going to be
able to give them to her.

"You okay?" Temper asks.

"Yeah, I'm fine, just a little nervous," I admit. "Mom
isn't going to make this easy on me, and I hate lying."
I'm a terrible liar. I usually just go quiet and not say
anything instead of making something up, which is a
dead giveaway.

"After what you took on two days ago, you're scared
of your mom?" he teases, squeezing my upper thigh.
"We've got this, all right?"

"She won't drill me when you're there," I say, pursing my lips. "She'll wait until you're gone and then ask
me all the questions. I know her and how she works.
It's not going to be pleasant."

"I can save you from a lot of things, Abbie, but your
mom's questioning, I'm afraid, is not one of them," he
says, amusement laced in his tone. "Just be as honest
as you need to be. We have nothing to hide."

I throw him a look. "Really? I've been kidnapped—by you—I've had a gun pointed at me multiple times... I could go on. These are all things I will not be honest about. I'm basically just going to play it like I was on holiday the whole time, finding myself or something like that."

Which is partly true.

I know who I am now more than I've ever known before.

"Valid points," he agrees. "Just say you had lots of adventures."

The second we pull up at my house, my mom runs out the front. I'm barely out of the car before I'm in her arms, and she's squeezing me tightly.

"Abbie, you're home," she says, smiling. She looks a little healthier than I left her, her cheeks fuller, her brown eyes sharp and filled with a mix of happiness and worry. "Thank God you're okay."

"I'm fine, Mom," I promise, letting her look over me. "Mom, this is Temper; Temper, this is my mom."

I know that they've interacted at Franks before, but that's not the same as properly meeting someone.

"Nice to officially meet you, ma'am," Temper says as he walks around to our side, offering her his hand. "I've heard lots about you."

"Have you now?" Mom replies, giving him a once-over as she shakes his hand. "Why don't you both come on in, and I'll make some tea?"

"Sounds good," I say, following her inside with Temper at my side.

"Ivy will be home soon," Mom says as we sit down on the couch. "She had to go into work, but said she will finish early."

"Okay," I reply. Mom disappears into the kitchen to make the tea, and I catch Temper staring around the room at all of my baby pictures.

"Man, you were the most adorable baby," he says, staring at the big picture of me hanging on the wall. I was about one then, with a thick head of hair and wearing a pretty white dress.

"How do you know that that's me?" I ask.

"The eyes, your smile," he replies, shrugging. "I'd know you anywhere."

"That's a bit cute."

"You're a bit cute," he says softly, eyes locked on me. "I love this house. I can picture you growing up here."

"Mom moved in here when I was a few months old, so it's the only house I've ever known," I admit.

I've been much luckier than Temper in regards to my childhood, and it's nice to be able to share that part of me. Having him here, sitting on the worn leather couch I used to play with my dolls on, brings him into my world, and lets him see a different side of me.

"You drink the tea first, just in case," he whispers to me, just before Mom steps back into the room.

Lip twitching, I wait for her to sit down and prepare myself for the questioning that's about to begin.

"So how was your trip? I'm still a little confused why you didn't even come and tell me or Ivy that you were going. You're not usually the spontaneous type," she says, pouring the tea for us all.

"It was a last-minute decision," I say, shrugging. "I should have told you. I know that, and I'm sorry."

Just like you should have told me who my dad was many years ago.

"Very unlike you," she murmurs, sliding me and Temper a mug each.

"Thank you," he says. "I think it was mostly my fault that she left so sudden. I was going on an adventure, and I asked her if she wanted to come with me. I made it pretty hard to say no."

Yeah, very hard, considering I was tied up.

"I see," Mom replies, lifting the tea to her lips and blowing the steam. "Well, I'm just glad that she's home."

"You're looking well," I say.

"I feel much better," she admits. "I've been taking the new medication, and to be honest, I feel stronger than I have in a long time."

"That's good." I smile. "How's Franks been doing?"

"Good. Ivy and Sierra have taken on your old shifts, and I'm in the process of hiring another part-time employee. We've had steady sales, so can't complain." She turns to Temper. "So... Temper, you're a biker. Is that how you earn your living?"

And here we go.

I should have introduced him as Tommy instead of Temper, but I just didn't think.

"I own a custom motorcycle shop," he replies. "So we sell custom bikes, but we can also customize the bikes people already have."

"I see," she replies, dragging out the word.

I don't know if she expected him to just say *I'm the president of a motorcycle club* or what, but she wasn't going to get it.

And technically, he's not lying to her.

"Well, I appreciate you bringing her back. It's been a lot of stress without her here—I've been worried sick. It was just so out of her character for her to just leave.

When I spoke to the police, they said there's nothing they could do because she's not a child, and has been in contact and stated she was fine."

"You called the police?" I ask, brow furrowing. "Seriously, Mom? I told you I was fine. I called you. I spoke to Ivy almost every day. I left you voice messages. Why would you call the police?"

"I was concerned," she says, lifting her chin, her gray-brown hair falling across her cheeks. "I'm your mother. I'm allowed to be concerned when you leave the bar with a random man and then suddenly decide not to come home."

"I get that, I do. But I'm also twenty-eight, Mom," I say gently. "And as you can see, I'm fine. Great, even. I'm happier than I've ever been, as a matter of fact."

"And I'm guessing this is all because of this man," she comments, looking at Temper. "First love always hits the hardest. How long are you staying in town?"

"Just a few days," he replies. "And then I'll head back to the city."

"Okay." She nods, glancing between the two of us.

We make some more small talk, and then Temper brings in my suitcase and goes to check in at the hotel. The second he leaves, just like I had guessed, Mom starts in on me.

"How old is he, Abbie? I think it's going to be so good for you when he leaves, and you can go back to your old life. You can return to college now and finish your degree. My health has improved a lot, and you don't need to worry about me being able to handle everything," she says, stroking my hair. "I don't know what you were thinking leaving town with a biker you just met, but I'm going to put it down to you having your little rebellious moment. Ivy had hers when she was younger, but you didn't, so I guess that's what this was."

"He's older than me," I admit. "I do want to go back to college."

Just in L.A., not here. I don't know how I'm going to break this to her, I know that she's not going to like it. Also there's the big elephant in the room, which is the whole Palmer thing, which she hasn't brought up, and neither have I.

For now.

Ivy comes home and wraps me in the biggest bear hug. "Oh my God, I've missed you so much."

"Me too," I say, smiling. "Thank you for covering for me and helping out. I owe you."

"Don't be silly," she says, waving her hand. "I think it showed me how much you'd taken on, and I should have been carrying more of that load."

"I'm the big sister," I say.

"Yeah, but we aren't kids anymore. I should be helping just as much, and trying to make things easier for you, too. You shouldn't feel like you need an escape so badly that you disappear in the middle of the night, so I'm sorry."

I hug her tighter. "You have nothing to be sorry about. I love you so much, Ivy. And I brought you presents back."

She grins. Mom, watching the whole exchange, makes a *tsk tsk* sound. "I don't think that's why she left, Ivy. I think she got a little infatuated with a certain biker."

Ivy and I share a look, and then she drags me to my bedroom and closes the door, demanding I tell her everything. So I start from the beginning, and fill her in.

Well, almost everything.

I leave out the dead body.

* * *

"Mom, I'm thinking about moving to California to finish school," I blurt out to her the next morning. There's no point beating around the bush. She needs to know what I'm thinking, and she needs to be okay with her firstborn finally leaving the nest, something which is long overdue.

Her eyes well up with tears. "We're a family, Abbie. You can't leave. We need you here."

"Mom, I'm old enough to move and live on my own and make my own decisions," I say in a gentle tone. "It's time for me to leave here. I've spoken to Ivy and she's happy for me. And we will all be visiting each other, and making time for each other. We're still family no matter what, but L.A. is where I want to be right now, and I need you to support that. I know you worry about me a lot, and you want me to be around always, but I think it's time for you to let me go and do my own thing. It doesn't mean I love you any less."

She sits there silently, sniffling. "I don't know, Abbie. I don't think that this is the best idea for you. You can finish your degree here—you don't need to move anywhere for a man. Why can't he move here to be with you if he wants to be with you so badly? Why do you have to make all of the changes?"

"I want to." I try to get through to her. "I love it there. I'm done with this small town. I want to be in the city. I've made new friends there, and it just feels like where I need to be right now. I know you hate change, but I've realized that I don't. I embrace it."

There would be absolutely no point asking Temper to move to this backwards town. I want to escape here, and I don't know how to get her to understand that without offending her.

"I love you, Mom, and I love Ivy, and that's not going to change. Me wanting to move and do my own thing doesn't mean that I'm going to just forget my family," I say, keeping my tone calm and gentle.

I can see her mind working. "When do you plan on leaving?"

"I don't know yet, maybe in a week or so? You guys don't need me at Franks anymore, Mom, you've got it all covered. You're not in bed resting anymore. You've sorted yourself out, and I'm so proud of you for doing that. I think me being gone was good for you, too, because you had to become a little more independent without me here looking after you. I just need to pack my stuff, and I'll enroll in college for next semester." Finishing my degree will be an absolute dream for me.

"A week?" she asks, scowling. "I don't know what you want me to say, Abbie. I've been so stressed without you here, and now you're going to tell me that you're moving away permanently? I just don't know how I'm supposed to be happy that my daughter is moving away from me. The crime in L.A. is off the charts—I was watching the news while you were gone, and it's not a safe city to be in. So many things can go wrong."

"So many things can go right, too. I'm living just out of L.A., Mom, so I'm not going to be in the hustle and bustle every day. You're making it personal, when it's not," I say, wishing she would just be happy for me. "I know that you feel anxious, but it's not fair for you to project that on me."

"How is it not personal?" she asks, shaking her head. "You're leaving us. That's personal. And I'm taking medication for my anxiety, Abbie. I just don't want my firstborn child to move away. Surely that's understandable?"

"Mom, she's twenty-eight, not sixteen," Ivy says, walking down the stairs and catching the end of our conversation. "You can't guilt trip her into staying here. That's not fair. She's old enough to live her life how she wants it; it's her life, not yours."

Thank God for baby sisters.

"This has nothing to do with you, Ivy. Your sister has changed so much in the time she's been gone. Imagine if she moves there! We won't even recognize her when she gets back."

Okay, that cut a little.

"It's called personal growth, Mom. She's growing into a better person. Stop trying to hold her back. And this has everything to do with me. I want to see my sister happy, and you should want to see Abbie happy too, even if it's not with her living under your roof," Ivy says, crossing her arms over her chest. "I'm going to go and visit with Abbie, so guess what? Sometimes you're going to have this place to yourself. Maybe you should take note and live a little, go on a vacation, go on a date, stop being so scared of the world all of the time. Maybe choose a man better than a drug dealer this time, though."

And there it is, the elephant I've been avoiding, but one apparently Ivy has no problem bringing up as a dig.

Mom opens her mouth then closes it, looking like a fish. "I'm not scared of the world. And fine, I made a mistake with Abbie's father, but that's why I didn't tell him I was pregnant. I left, because I knew it was best for Abbie, and I didn't want her growing up around that environment. And now she's gone and found herself a criminal biker anyway, so she's basically put herself into the same environment."

"I don't think those two things are the same," I say, scowling. "And Grayson told me he never knew you were pregnant, but when exactly did he find out about me then?"

She stills, as if realizing her mistake. "When I called him to ask him to go and check on you."

I blink slowly, my lips parting. "So you're telling me…you called him up, and told him he had a grown-ass daughter that he never knew about, and that he needs to go looking for me because I was alone in L.A. with a bunch of bikers?"

"Basically," she says, lifting her chin. "I did what was best for you. He wasn't the type of man to play the father role, and I should have never gotten pregnant by him; it was an accident. Not that I regret you, Abbie. Both of you girls are my greatest gifts, but I wish I gave you both better fathers, and that's on me. I protected you, okay? I did what I needed to."

I don't even know what to say right now, but I feel bad for Grayson. I just assumed he found out after my mother left him about me and chose not to be in my life. But he never knew. Maybe he would have stepped up if he was actually given the option to be a father.

To know he was one.

But she took that away from him.

"What did he say when you told him about me?" I press, needing to know these details now. I'm angry at her, so angry, but it's not going to change anything now. This has really showed me a side of her that I don't like at all.

"He was shocked," she admits, wincing. "Very angry. He didn't believe me at first, but then he did, especially when I told him your birthdate and sent him a picture of you. You have his—"

"Eyes. I know."

"How do you know?" my mom asks.

"Because I've met with him. A couple of times now," I admit, jaw tight. "Could you imagine if the roles were reversed and someone did this to you? You'd be devastated. I don't know how you justified this, Mom. How did you sleep at night knowing you were keeping me a secret?"

"I was doing what was best," she says, and I can see in her eyes that she truly believes that. "And you met him? Neither of you mentioned that."

Yeah, and I wonder why. She is the one who kept us apart—why would we go running to her with any information?

"He deserved to know," I tell her, my voice raising. "If he wasn't good enough to be a father, then you should have been more responsible when you were sleeping with him. But you weren't, and half of my DNA is his. You don't get to play God and decide who gets to be in my life."

"He's a drug dealer!" she screams back at me. "Yes, I should have been more responsible, but I wasn't, and I wasn't about to bring you down to his level."

"At least he has been somewhat honest," I fire back at her, watching her flinch. "You can say whatever you want about his character, but it's not him who has lied to me for my entire life."

Just when I thought I couldn't be shocked anymore, the woman comes up with this information.

Chapter Twenty-Nine

"Why didn't he just tell you that when you saw him?" Temper asks, arms around me as he strokes my back. "I don't get it. He easily could have told you he only just found out about you, and then you wouldn't have been so angry."

"I don't know. Maybe he doesn't want to be a dad. Maybe he was in shock, which is fair enough. I'm sure it's not every day a woman from your past calls you and tells you, 'By the way, you have a grown child.' And let's not forget his...career choices. He probably knows he's not role model material."

The whole thing is just sad. It's probably no one's fault. I mean, Mom should have been honest, but she did what she thought was best at the time, and that's all there is to it. There's no point thinking about the what-ifs. It is what it is.

"Maybe we misjudged him," Temper thinks out loud. "What if he's not so bad as we've made him out to be? I mean, look at the reputation the Knights get, and we're not all bad."

"You're not bad to the people on your side," I remind him, arching my brow.

"And what if he's the same?"

I pause for a moment, considering. "He might be," I agree. "But according to what you have all heard, he's the main drug distributor in the city. That is not a good man. That's a man who gives no fucks about his actions, or the pain he causes people. That's a coldhearted man who sees money, and that's it."

"You're probably right…"

But maybe I'm not.

Maybe I'm being a hypocrite, and maybe I'm holding him to a higher standard than I am holding everyone else to.

"When did things get so damn difficult?" I groan, burying my face in his chest. "I'm just going to stay here forever and never move again. I'm done with being an adult."

His chest moves as he laughs. "It will be fine; the worst of it is over. You told your mom you're moving, which was the hardest part. Tomorrow I'll help you pack so you don't have too much to do, and then I'll head home. You spend a week with your family, and then I'll come back to pick you up."

"I can just drive there. I need to bring my car anyway," I say, raising my eyes to his. "There's no point you driving all the way back here."

"You sure?" he asks, frowning. "Nah, I want to come and get you. After not seeing you for a whole week, I'm going to be going crazy."

"You'll survive," I tease, pushing off his body, and sit on the edge of the bed. The hotel room is identical to the one we had our first date in, which is pretty cute, and brings back those memories. "Have you spoken to Saint? Anything happened back home?"

"Back home, hey?" he murmurs, smile in his voice.

"You know what I mean," I say, laughing as he pulls me back down on top of him. I guess I have already started seeing the clubhouse as my new home, without even realizing it.

"I like that you're already thinking of it as your home," he whispers in my ear, sending goose bumps all over my skin. "The thought of you living there makes me so happy, you have no idea."

"Good," I say, and moan as he places a soft, tingling kiss on the side of my neck.

"And everything is fine back home. No drama," he assures me, kissing me again. "Life is probably waiting for us to return before it throws some more shit at us."

"You know what they say, you're only given what you can handle," I breathe, arching my neck as he continues to torture me.

"Well then, we can handle anything."

I feel like we're definitely going to test that theory.

After packing up everything I want to take back with me and loading some of it into Temper's car, we go sightseeing, and do a hike together up one of the mountains.

"This is our first time doing exercise together," I say, turning back to point at him. "Besides boxing and sex."

"I was about to say." He smirks, placing his hands on my hips. "I don't know, though—we've done a lot of running into cars to get away from being shot."

"That's true," I admit, panting as we make it to the top. "How are you not dying right now? Your stamina is insane." I cover his mouth with my hand. "Don't even say anything."

Resting on my knees, I catch my breath before looking

out at the beautiful view, the reason why I had to walk for over two hours. "I forgot how amazing it is up here."

The area is unusual and gorgeous, especially amidst the desert. Temper looks out over all the greenery, the lush forest, the green sky and the large lake. "Definitely worth the trek."

He wraps his arm around me and pulls me closer to his side, and we just take in the view, and the moment. It's nice to think that this is just the beginning, we have so much to experience together, so many firsts, and many more adventures.

"I'm glad we decided to do this," he admits, taking a picture of the view on his phone. "I don't know why you thought staying in bed naked together instead was a better idea."

"That was you," I say with narrowed eyes. "You're the fiend here."

"Can you blame me? Have you seen you? Keeping my hands off you is a hard task, and sometimes I seem to fail at it. Plus, a week, remember."

"How can I forget? We should take a selfie," I tell him, pulling out my phone. "Can you take it? You're so tall I probably won't even be able to get your head into the shot." He takes the camera from me, and takes not one, but a few photos, which I appreciate. "Thanks. We look cute together."

"You're only realizing that now?" he asks.

We have some water and a snack then head back down the mountain. The closer we get to the end, the sooner it means he'll be leaving without me. I will miss him, but I'll see him soon enough. I only have one thing on my mind right now, and that's getting him back for the prank he pulled on me in the car.

He's not going to know what hit him.

* * *

In the middle of the night, dressed in all black, armed with a flashlight and my sidekick sister, I drive to the hotel and park next to Temper's car.

"This is going to take a long time," I admit, wincing. "But going to be so worth it. He's going to flip out. I wish I was going to be here in the morning to see his face."

"Definitely going to be worth it," she responds, handing me a huge pack of Post-its. We both get out of the car and start to cover his entire car in little multicolored Post-its.

"Okay, this is going to take longer than I thought." I groan, but smirk when I see how it's starting to look. "I'd be so pissed if someone did this to my car."

"It's pretty funny," my sister says, laughing to herself.

Once we're all done, on the one that covers his door handle, I write:

Checkmate.

Giggling, we get back into our car and speed home.

Before I even wake up properly, I can hear my mom's and Temper's voices. Groaning, I roll out of bed and head downstairs. They haven't had a chance to have a conversation without me, so I don't know if I should intervene and save him or let them just have it out once and for all.

"You know, you could tell her this isn't a good idea," my meddling mother says to him. "She's safest here, with her family."

"She's old enough to make her own decisions," Temper says to her respectfully. "And I'd love to have her near L.A. with me, so I'm not going to talk her out of that. If she told me that she wanted to stay here, then I'd respect her decision either way. It's whatever she wants and whatever will make her happy. I know you're sad that she's leaving, but you aren't losing her. She'll visit and stay in contact, and it's only a few hours away. It's not like she's moving to a different country."

"She's blinded," Mom replies, and it's then I realize that she's not actually listening to what we're saying. She can't see out of her own views and feelings, and she doesn't actually care how I feel about anything.

Stepping down the rest of the stairs, I walk into the kitchen, where they're both sitting, having coffee. "Good morning."

"Morning," Temper says.

"Coffee?" they both ask me at the same time.

"Yes, please," I say, lip twitching as Mom quickly goes to make me one. Temper opens his arms and gives me a big hug. "You all packed and ready to go?" I ask, squeezing him tightly.

"Yeah. Is there anything else of yours you want me to fit into the car? I have lots of space."

I nod. "Yeah, I have a few boxes that I've left in my room. If you could take them, that would be awesome."

"I'll go and get them now," he murmurs, kissing my temple.

While he heads up and down the stairs, retrieving the boxes, I have my coffee and then follow him to his car. "I'm going to miss you," I say. "Call me when you get home safely?"

"I will," he promises, looking down at me and scanning my eyes. "And let me know if you want me to come and pick you up, all right? I don't love the idea of you driving there all alone."

"I'll be fine," I say, rolling my eyes. I know he doesn't like it, but I like that he flat out doesn't try to tell me no, you can't do that. He lets me make my own decisions, and I know that it's hard for someone like him, who is used to deciding everyone's fate and having the last word on all decisions.

He kisses me, cupping my face, his mouth telling me without words how much he truly is going to miss me. My eyes flutter back open as he pulls away, and I reach out for him as he gets into his car.

"I love you," he says.

"I love you, too," I reply, watching as he drives away.

I'm going to miss him, but I know that the next time I see him, I'm going to be living with him, and that is huge. I'm also excited to spend some quality time with my family before I move away.

Sighing, I head back into my room, only to find a huge spider, the size of my fist, on my bed.

I start screaming loudly, running out of my room and into my sister's, who was fast asleep but is now awake and standing on her bed in nothing but her underwear.

"What is it? What is it?" she asks, putting her hands up like she's about to fight someone.

"There's a spider on my bed. It's huge. Can you catch it and put it outside?" I ask, covering my cheeks with my palms.

She throws on her robe and grabs a container, then steps into my room. "Holy fuck, that thing is massive. It's basically Aragog."

She makes a little sound of hesitation, then steps closer to the bed and places the container on the spider.

"Wait a minute," she says, tilting her head to the side.

Lifting the container, she takes the spider in her hand, and throws it on me.

Screaming, I run out of the room, ignoring her high-pitched laughter.

"It's plastic," she calls out to me, still laughing.

"What?" I ask, coming back into the room. "It's fake?" She nods. "Fuck," I say out loud.

And then it all hits me.

The Post-its.

He must have placed the spider on my bed when he went up to get the boxes.

"The bastard got the last word in the end," I say.

She laughs some more.

Chapter Thirty

My mom spends the next few days trying to get in my head and make me change my mind about leaving. It doesn't work, and I think she realizes that, because she starts to give up.

"I'm going to miss you," she says one morning, still in her pajamas, her hair mussed from sleep. "I've been thinking about everything that you've said to me, and you're right. You're old enough to do your own thing, and I shouldn't project my worries on you. You're just so fearless, Abbie, and it scares me. I don't know what I'd do if something happened to you."

"I'm going to be fine, Mom," I promise, taken aback by her admission. I truly wasn't sure if she was going to come around and make this easier on me, or if she was going to let me leave without us on good terms, which would have made me feel really bad. "I have a man who will do anything for me, and wonderful new friends, and I'm finally going to follow my dreams of finishing my degree."

"I'm proud of you," she admits, smiling sadly. "I don't think I'm ever going to stop worrying about you, but I'm proud of you."

"Thanks, Mom," I say, giving her a big hug. "It

means a lot to me. I'll still call you all the time, and come see you when I can. Or you can come and see me. Okay?"

"Okay," she breathes, rubbing my back.

It's nice for her to finally see things from my perspective, and not just from her own, and I really appreciate her doing that because I know how hard it must have been for her to let go of her own worries and insecurities.

I finish packing my room, and I spend most of my time with Ivy. I'm really going to miss her, but I know that we will still see each other, and it's exciting to think of her coming out to visit me. We even plan to do a trip to New York together. I have enough money saved that it will last me a few months, and it gives me plenty of time to find a job, which saves me a lot of stress. Perks of living at home for so long, I was able to put away a good-sized chunk of money to use for whatever I please.

Temper calls me every night, and sends me good morning messages every morning. I look forward to them every day, but it's also nice that during the day we do our own thing and aren't spending all of our time constantly chatting and ignoring everyone else around us.

When it's time for me to drive back, Ivy sits on the hood of my car, her cute little sad face breaking my heart. "This is the end of an era," she says, wrapping her arms around herself.

"When can you come and visit me? Next week?" I ask, giving her a big hug.

"When I have my college break," she says, resting her cheek on my shoulder. "I think Mom would have a heart attack if I left right away."

"You're probably right."

Mom rushes outside, containers of food in her hands. "I packed something for you to eat on the drive over, and some extras for Temper."

"Thanks, Mom," I say, taking the food from her, and I put it in the passenger's seat. "I'll call you both when I get there."

Mom gives me a long hug, and when she lets me go, there are tears in her eyes. "I love you."

"I love you, too," I say to her, giving Ivy another hug, and then get into my car. I'm moving to a town near L.A.

To live in a clubhouse full of bikers.

And I'm going to love every second of it.

Chapter Thirty-One

One Month Later

Glancing around our bedroom, I smile at the final touches: the potted plants in the corner adding a little greenery, the bookshelf, the chair and the framed canvas photo of Temper and me above the bed.

"Looks beautiful," Temper says, standing behind me. "More homey than it's ever been. But I think that's just because you're here, not because of all the fancy shit you've put in."

I rest my hands on his as they come around my waist. "I think it feels homey, too."

Sometimes, home is a person instead of a place.

I've loved my first few weeks of officially living in the clubhouse. I've started my new job at Grapevine, a cool bar that I love, even if Temper usually sends someone in to check on me if he can't do it himself. I love hanging with Skylar, Izzy and Ariel, and I love coming home to Temper every night. I took a gamble moving out here, but I don't regret it, not one bit. I've made sure to call my mom and keep in touch, and Ivy is going to be visiting for a week very soon.

Temper pulls me down on the fresh mustard-yellow

bedding. It's late, and I can't think of anything better than undressing and crawling under these sheets. He assists in undressing me, then himself, and pulls the sheets down.

As soon as I'm under the covers, naked, Temper presses his body against mine, and starts to kiss me, massage my back and have as much skin on skin contact as possible. He kisses all over my body, teasing me for what feels like ages until he finally goes down on me, licking my clit how he knows I like it, sliding his tongue and hitting just the right spot. Just when I'm about to come, though, he stops, pulling back, leaving me wanting.

"Temper," I grumble, spreading my thighs, arching my back, begging for more, but he continues to take his time, now licking and kissing my inner thighs, which have started quivering.

Instead of going where I want him to, he moves back up to my breasts, dragging his teeth over my nipples before sucking them deep into his mouth. Moaning, I let my head fall back, my toes curling, my fingers digging into the mattress.

When he moves back down, I'm so wet and turned on that I think that even a look from him is going to push me over the edge. He slides a finger inside my sex first, then another, before finally lowering his mouth on me.

As the tip of his tongue touches my clit, I come instantly, speaking in tongues, saying God knows what. All I know is that I'm pretty loud, but I couldn't stop myself if I tried, each wave of pleasure more delicious than the last.

He rings every ounce of the orgasm out of me, until there's no way I can take anymore, and only then does he lazily slide into me, kissing my lips and slowly making love to me.

"I love you," he says against my lips.

"I love you too," I whisper back, smiling.

When I get a text message from Grayson, I reply instantly. He's been wanting to see me for a while now, but I've always been busy at work, or spending time with the MC.

Grayson: Your mom called me again. She said you seem happy, which is good. Do you want to have coffee sometime this week? It's hard knowing you're so close now, but we still haven't seen each other again.

Why is Mom still calling him?

Abbie: Mom told me that you never knew about me until recently. I'm sorry about the whole situation. I assumed that you knew and just didn't care. Sure, I guess we could have coffee. Next week, though?

I may not have been intentionally avoiding him, but I know too much time has passed without me getting a few things off my chest. There are things that I've been thinking about ever since I learned the truth about him.

Grayson: I understand if you're wary about getting to know me. Yes, I only just found out about you. I don't have any other children, and if I knew about you I would have liked to be involved in your life. It's a shame I wasn't given that option, but it's all in the past now and we can't change that. We can only control where we go from here. Next week sounds perfect.

"What are you going to do?" Skylar asks when I tell her about it. "Just get to know him? The whole thing is so weird."

"I don't know. What do you think I should do?" I ask.

"I think you should talk to him, and ask him, 'What the fuck, Daddy?'" she says. "Get some answers from him. Find out who he really is, because right now, we have no idea."

"Okay, never call him Daddy again," I say, wrinkling my nose.

"Yeah, no," Crow concurs, shaking his head as he steps into the room. "A woman did call me that in the bedroom last week, though. It was hot."

"Oversharing is a thing," I say to him.

"Don't you have Temper's name saved in your phone as Daddy Temper?" Skylar reminds me, laughing out loud.

Crow winks. "See, hot."

"Thanks for that, Skylar," I say, trying to keep a straight face. "No, really, thank you."

"What are friends for?" she replies, smirking. "But seriously, though, I don't think Grayson's someone you want on your bad side—he's clearly a master liar and actor. I like to think I'm a good judge of character, and he had me fooled. That being said, just because he lied to me doesn't mean I have anything against the guy. He never treated me badly and I don't really see how him lying to me all these years really hurt me in the long run. I just think you should be careful."

"Yeah," I say, and I can tell Skylar sees the trepidation in my eyes.

"If it makes you feel better, I saw the way he looked at you, and I think he truly does care about you."

I nod. "I don't feel like he has ill intentions toward me. I don't think he'll intentionally harm me."

"Then give him a real chance," she suggests, tapping her index finger on her chin. "I think you'll gain something from him. He's not ideal father material, but hey, who are we to judge?"

I smile and duck my head, because she's right.

At the end of the day, he's still my father, and that means something to me.

Chapter Thirty-Two

"Why the hell is there a million packages here?" I ask, stepping around them as I get home from my first shift at the Grapevine.

"The girls' online shopping orders arrived," Chains says, studying the boxes. "What the hell did they buy? An entire store?"

"It sure looks that way," I say, walking to the kitchen. "Where's Temper?"

"He got a call and left," Chains says, following me.

"How was work?" Crow asks when he spots me. "You finished early?"

"Yeah, we were overstaffed, so they said I could leave early," I explain, jumping up on the countertop. "I saw your girlfriend there again tonight, too."

"Who?" Chains asks, smirking at Crow. "You have a girlfriend?"

"She's being sarcastic. It's just some chick who thinks I have beer-flavored come or something. I don't know, she's been trying to sleep with me ever since I was dating Aisha, and it's her friend."

"She's a Stage Five clinger," I admit to Chains. "How about you? How's your love life going these days?"

After spending more time with Chains, he's started

opening up a bit. He's a very blunt, forward person, and he doesn't really follow social cues like a normal person would. Once you get to know him, though, he's actually a good guy. He just hides it well.

"Nonexistent. I like sex, but I don't know if it's worth the pillow talk and hugging they want from me afterward," he says, shrugging.

"Savage," I whisper, wrinkling my nose. "My sister Ivy is coming for a visit next week. Neither of you look at her, please and thank you."

"Why would you do that?" Crow asks, shaking his head and groaning, tapping his hand to his forehead. "Did you just make her forbidden?"

"No."

"Yes, you did. You told me to stay away from her, which made her forbidden, which made me interested," the bastard says.

I pick up an apple from the fruit bowl and throw it at him, but he ducks. "I'll kill you. Are you saying if I didn't warn you off her then you wouldn't have been interested? Because she's a stunning girl, way prettier than me."

"I don't know, maybe, but the fact that you made her forbidden…" He makes a growling sound.

I throw a banana at him, and it hits him in the face.

"I won't be the only one getting a banana in my face soon—"

I throw a pineapple at him this time, and I aim lower.

His scream is so worth it.

"Say forbidden one more time and next time it's going to be a watermelon," I threaten.

"I didn't realize you were so violent," he says from the floor, cupping his nuts.

"Really? She shot Georgia in the foot," Chains reminds him, then picks up the banana from the floor and starts eating it.

"Hey," I say when Temper appears. "Where did you go?"

"Your father just called," he admits, coming to the counter and standing between my legs.

"Why would he call you?" I ask, frowning. "Is he okay? Did something happen?"

"No, nothing happened, to him anyway. He asked me to open the gate to let him in."

"He's here?" I ask, brow furrowing. He lifts me off the table and I follow him to the front door.

"Yeah, said he has something to tell us."

I'm confused, but curious. Temper said nothing is wrong, but it's not like Grayson just drops into the clubhouse to have coffee.

I stand at the open door while Temper opens the gate, Grayson's BMW parking amongst the Knights' motorcycles and cars. When he gets out, he looks so out of place here, dressed in a sharp black suit.

"Hey," I say as he approaches. "Fancy seeing you here."

"A place I never thought I'd be," he admits. "Is there somewhere we can talk?"

I nod, and lead him through the house and out the back door, Temper close behind us. As we all sit outside, I ask him if he wants a beer.

"No thank you," he replies, eyes softening. "I was wondering if you could tell Skylar to come here, because she needs to be here to hear this."

"Of course," I say, and send her a quick message. As far as I know, she's here and in her room, but a text is still the quickest way to contact anyone in this place. She replies that she will be out in a second.

If Skylar needs to be here, I can think of only one person who ties us all together.

"Is this about Georgia? Did she say something else about me? Is she going to come into work and fly kick me or something?"

"There will be no fly kicking," he replies in low, serious tone.

Skylar opens the sliding door and sticks her head outside. "Hey, is everything okay?" Her eyes widen when she sees Grayson sitting there. "Hello, there's a face I didn't expect to see."

"Hello, Skylar," Grayson replies.

I pull out the chair next to me, and she drops into it, a concerned expression on her face. "Okay, you guys are scaring me now. What has happened?"

"It's your mom," he says before clearing his throat. "She's dead."

Everything and everyone goes silent.

Skylar wraps her arms around herself, brows drawing together. "How?"

I'm wondering the exact same thing. I look at Temper, whose expression is blank, his eyes already on me, watching me.

Grayson said he would take care of things for me.

He wouldn't have, would he?

"Car crash," Grayson says, reaching out and touching Skylar's shoulder. "They found her body this morning near her hotel. She must have been driving home from somewhere."

I don't know what to say right now. I mean, I'm not

sad by any means. This woman was a threat to everything that I love.

"Are you okay?" I ask Skylar, wrapping my arm around her and offering my support. I can't imagine how she's feeling.

"I will be," she replies with a sad smile.

I'm still trying to wrap my head around the whole thing, and Georgia isn't even my mother. This woman was quite the enigma, and nobody could bring her down because of who she was, but now she simply dies in a car crash?

"I don't even know what to say." She sighs, rubbing her face. "Was it really an accident?"

She's asking Grayson what I want to know but didn't want to ask in front of her.

Grayson nods, but I notice that he doesn't look at her. "The cops said there was something wrong with her brakes."

"I see. I think I'm in shock," she whispers, rubbing her eyes, and takes a deep breath. Her hands are shaking a little, and I hate to see her like this. I send Saint a message to tell him what's happened and that Skylar needs him right now.

"I know she was horrible to me," she continues, as if she feels like she has to explain her grief. Her eyes start to tear up, but she blinks away the pain, composing herself.

"You're allowed to feel however you want," I assure her, stroking her back. "You don't have to justify anything, Skylar. We're here for you, and there's no judgment there, okay? We love you. And we will all help you get through this."

She nods and gives me a small, grateful smile. Her

eyes are full of pain, confusion and regret. Even in her death, Georgia messes with her daughter's head. "I know. Thank you for coming here and telling me, Neville. I mean…Grayson."

"Of course," he replies, sounding defeated.

Georgia was evil, cruel and psychotic, but she raised a compassionate, strong daughter, and for that the world can be thankful. And at the end of the day Skylar only had one mother, and even if she didn't turn out how anyone had wished, I think she'll always mourn the loss of her.

"At least we don't have to worry anymore," Skylar says, smiling sadly. "Everyone I love is safer now, and I'm so sorry you all had to deal with everything she put us through."

"You never did anything wrong," Grayson says. "You have nothing to apologize for. If anything I should be saying sorry to you, for not stepping in earlier."

Skylar ducks her head. "You were always kind to me. No one could save me from her. She was my mother."

"I should have tried," Grayson whispers, looking away.

Swallowing hard, I take a deep breath and reach for Skylar's hand. "You're going to be okay. We're all going to be okay now."

Saint arrives, swooping in and taking Skylar away. I know that she's going to need his comfort, and we can't imagine how difficult and confusing this moment must be for her. No one cares that Georgia's dead, but we care about Skylar, and what she's feeling right now. But we're going to be here for her, like we always have, like her mother never was.

Some families are made from blood, and some are created by loyalty.

Some of us are lucky enough to have both, and if you do, then you're truly blessed.

"It's weird having you in here," I admit to my father, giving him a hug. A few beers later, and we're all sitting around still discussing everything that has happened. "How are *you* feeling?"

It has to be a bittersweet feeling for him. He was married to this woman, and loved her, even if it was in some twisted way.

And now, because of me, he could have had his hand in killing her.

He sighs before answering. "I'm okay, don't you worry about me. At least I know that you're safe now."

There's pain in his eyes, and he can't hide that from me.

"I'm sorry," I say quietly, so that the others can't hear. He's putting me first, like a father should do, and I'm grateful for that. I still don't like seeing him hurt, though.

"So what really happened?" I ask, not buying the whole faulty brakes thing.

"Her car crashed into a tree," Grayson says, giving nothing away in those familiar eyes. "She was the only passenger. The hotel manager found her and called the cops. She must have been speeding, or drunk or something."

"Okay," I say with narrowed eyes, not sure what to believe. "So she's really gone, huh?"

Grayson nods, glances up at the sky, and then takes a deep drink of his beer.

The witch is dead.

Epilogue

Three Months Later

"So, I'm throwing a poker fund-raiser for the children's hospital, and you're invited," I say to Grayson, over our usual weekly coffee. Our relationship has been growing. We started seeing each other sporadically, but after getting to know him more, I realized that he's a genuinely fascinating guy. So we began to make weekly coffee dates where he'd tell me something about himself and I'd tell him about something from my life. Something he missed out on. And now I'm at the point where I feel comfortable enough to allow him to be more involved in my life than just over a cappuccino.

"I'll be there," he says, studying me. "You starting to run the place, huh?"

"I'm not running anything," I reply, rolling my eyes. "But as Temper's girlfriend, I don't want to be sitting there and doing nothing. I have a role and things I can be doing to help the club. I want to give back to the community, and maybe change some people's minds about us."

It's hard being the newest to the group and standing

next to their leader and being his old lady, but I'm trying my best. I think the fund-raiser will be a success, and slowly I can start doing more and more things for the club and taking on that role.

"If anyone can do that, it's you," he says, smiling, amber eyes on me.

I never asked him what hand he played with Georgia's death, and he's never brought it up. But I have to wonder if…no, I won't let myself go there.

All I know is that without her around, I feel safer, and less on edge, and even Skylar seems like a weight has been lifted off her shoulders.

Three Months After That

"How was your first day?" Temper asks me, standing by his bike, looking sexy as hell in light jeans and a dark top. Everyone on campus is looking at us, not that I care, but this man always knows how to make an entrance.

"It was great, even better now that you're here," I say, kiss him and climb on the back of his bike.

Words can't express how happy I am to be back on track with following my dreams. I've taken on fewer shifts at the Grapevine so I can concentrate on my studies, spend time with Temper and the MC, and also get to know my father.

I've decided I want to be the best lawyer in the city. I can picture it now. Me in a white suit, Temper at my side, dressed in black leather, opposites, somehow balancing each other out. The Knights breaking the law and me protecting them. I laugh to myself at the thought.

Instead of riding straight home, Temper takes me to a restaurant near the beach and tells me he has a surprise for me.

Always with the surprises.

After we finish our meal, we take a walk down to the sand. "You want to go skinny dipping or something, don't you?"

"Something like that." He laughs, taking my hand.

I stop walking when I see what's in front of me. On the beach, just before the sand meets the water, is the whole MC, standing in a row.

Grayson is there, too.

And Ivy.

And even my mom.

"What's going on?" I ask Temper, who leads me down to them, down a path on the sand marked by a trail of sunflowers.

When he gets down on one knee, my hand flies to my mouth, shock and happiness hitting me.

"Abigail Redmond, I've loved you from the moment I saw you. You are my soul mate, my true love, and you make me a better person just by being around you. You are the light to my dark, you bring laughter and happiness to my soul and I want to spend the rest of my life with you. Will you marry me?"

"Yes, of course I will," I say, tears dropping from my eyes.

He slides a beautiful pear-shaped diamond on my finger, while everyone cheers and claps for us.

"It's stunning," I say, kissing him, and wipe my tears. "I love you so much."

He cups my face with his hands and rests his forehead against mine. "Just me and you, against the world, forever."

And the rest of the MC, of course.

Forever.

* * * * *

*Reviews are an invaluable tool when it comes to
spreading the word about great reads.
Please consider leaving an honest review for this
or any of Carina Press's other titles that you've read
on your favorite retailer or review site.*

*For more information on books
by Chantal Fernando,
please visit her website
at www.authorchantalfernando.com.*

Acknowledgments

A big thank-you to Carina Press for working with me on the Knights of Fury MC series!

Thank you to Kimberly Brower, my amazing agent, for having my back in all things. We make a great team, always have and always will.

Natalie Ram—I miss you, bestie! It's hard doing life without you, but I know you are just a call away. I love you. Thank you for always reading my work and supporting me, even though I know how busy you are.

Amo Jones—Thank you for always being there when I need someone to talk to, for the badass writing sprints and for encouraging me to be the best writer I can be. You just get me, and finding someone that does that is so rare. I love you, wifey.

Brenda Travers—Thank you so much for all that you do to help promote me. I am so grateful. You go above and beyond and I appreciate you so much.

Ari—You are one of the best souls I have ever met. You are kind, generous and I'm so lucky to have you in my life. Thank you for always caring about me. I love you!

Tenielle—Baby sister, I don't know where I'd be without you. Thanks for all you do for me and the boys;

we all adore you and appreciate you. I might be older, but you inspire me every day. When I grow up, I want to be like you.

Christian—Thank you for always being there for me, and for accepting me just the way I am. I always tell you how lucky you are to have me in your life, but the truth is I'm pretty damn lucky myself. I appreciate all you do for me and the boys. I love you.

To my three sons, my biggest supporters—thank you for being so understanding, loving and helpful. I'm so proud of the men you are all slowly becoming, and I love you all so very much. I hope that watching me work hard every day and following my dreams inspires you all to do the same. Nothing makes me happier than being your mama.

And Chookie—no, I love you more.

And to my readers, thank you for loving my words. I hope this book is no exception.

About the Author

New York Times, Amazon and *USA TODAY* bestselling author Chantal Fernando is thirty-two years old and lives in Western Australia.

Lover of all things romance, Chantal is the author of the bestselling books *Dragon's Lair*, *Maybe This Time* and many more.

When not reading, writing or daydreaming, she can be found enjoying life with her three sons and family.

Now Available from Carina Press and Chantal Fernando

New York Times *bestselling author of the Knights of Fury MC series Chantal Fernando is back with trouble in the form of a renegade.*

Read on for an excerpt from Renegade

"You have got to be kidding me," I groan, slamming my hands down on the steering wheel in frustration. After a week of nothing but bad luck, from locking myself out of my house to smashing the screen on my phone, I shouldn't be surprised that my car has decided to die on me just as I'm about to leave for a road trip to visit my nine-months-pregnant sister, but I am.

After getting out of the car and opening the hood, pretending like I know what I'm supposed to be looking for, I realize that I don't.

Shit.

My car is old, but it's been reliable up until now, and I'm pissed this is the moment it has chosen to be disloyal. I'm going to have to call a mechanic and hope that it can be fixed right now, or I'm screwed.

I type *cheap local mechanics* into my phone when I hear the familiar sound of a motorcycle rumble, a sound I've gotten so used to that it is just background noise. I've been living near the Knights of Fury Motorcycle Club for a few years now, and even though there's a block of vacant land between us, I still call them my neighbors.

My mother and sister told me I was crazy for knowingly moving next to a bunch of bikers, but my house was such a good price, I couldn't turn it down. I suppose I have them to thank for that, because no one else wanted to live near them. Besides, what really is a motorcycle club? I suspect it sounds a lot more nefarious than it really is.

And it hasn't been all bad. Our interactions have been limited to the casual head nod as they ride by. There was one moment where a woman was in a pickle and dropped in to use my phone. There's been no crime in the area, and I surprisingly feel pretty safe.

I start dialing a mechanic and the rumble gets louder as a black Harley comes to a stop behind my car. It's kind of been our unspoken rule that the bikers and I live harmoniously, but don't really engage, so it surprises me when someone gets off the bike and removes his helmet.

Hello, Mr. Biker. He's one good-looking biker, that's for sure. Dark hair, dark eyes, stubble and a tall, built body dressed in all black. He slowly approaches, eyes on my car.

"Need some help?" he says, his deep timbre sending a shiver down my spine.

"That would be great." I'm desperate at this point, especially when the phone rings with no answer from mechanic number one. "I don't know what happened. It only made it down the road before it just stopped."

He comes to stand next to me, and fiddles with the engine before getting in the car and trying to start it to no avail. "I'm going to have to take it in to the clubhouse," he says, frowning. "We can fix it and get it back to you ASAP."

"I appreciate the offer," I say, shifting on my feet

as he stares at me. "But I'm kind of supposed to be in Vegas today."

I'm going to have to call the last person I want to call to ask if I can borrow his car.

My father.

Ugh.

"Vegas? We're actually heading that way ourselves. We can give you a ride, if you want," he says, shrugging. "I'm Renny, by the way." He holds out his hand for me to shake.

Renny?

I vaguely remember hearing this name before. Maybe it was when that woman used my phone.

"Isabella," I reply, shaking the tattooed hand. It's big, yet warm and soft, despite the calluses on it.

"I know who you are," he murmurs. "You helped Skylar when she needed it." Skylar, that was her name! "Now why don't you let us return the favor? It's the least we can do."

"I didn't really do anything," I say, surprised he remembers something so small. I mean I let her inside to use my phone, and that's about it. Anyone would do that for someone that they see is visibly in distress.

"You helped. That day..." He pauses with a far-off look on his face. "It was a tough day. We lost someone important and you helping her... Well, it meant a lot. So thank you."

"You're welcome," I say, knowing that arguing would be pointless. "What are neighbors for, right?"

He grins at that, a little dimple popping up on the right side of his cheek, distracting me. "So what about my offer. Do you want to hitch a ride to Vegas?"

His offer sounds tempting, but I really don't know

these men, and I'd rather drive there by myself. Even if that means I have to call my dad.

Who am I kidding? While I wouldn't feel comfortable driving to Vegas with Renny and his friends, I'd probably still choose that option over asking Dad for help.

My phone rings, bringing me back to reality, especially when my sister's name pops up on the screen.

Shit.

"Ariel, hello?" I say, raising a finger to Renny apologetically. I turn my back a little for privacy, glancing down at my shoes, silently praying that everything is okay.

"Izzy, have you left? I'm in labor, it wasn't just Braxton Hicks. You need to be here now!" she says in a panic. "The way these contractions are coming on..." She starts to scream in pain, and I hold the phone away from my ear, wincing. "Fuck!"

Man, I am never having a baby if that is what I have to go through. My older sister is one of the strongest women I know, and she has a high pain threshold, so anything that makes her sound like that gets a nope from me.

"I'm leaving now," I promise, turning back to Renny. "I'll be there as soon as I can, Ariel. I love you."

"I love you, too," she says before hanging up.

I weigh my options and the likelihood that I will make it to Vegas in time. I may not know Renny, but I promised Ariel I would be there for the birth of her child. My niece or nephew. And I will not let her down.

"So when are you leaving?" I ask before I can give any more thought to what I am doing. I need to go, and I need to go now. It's a five-hour drive, and maybe, just maybe, I will make it before the baby's head crowns and ruins Ariel's vagina.

"Was going to be in an hour or so, but we can make it right now," he says, pulling out his phone. "I'll tell the men."

"Just how many men are we traveling with?" I ask as he types out a text message. "And what about my suitcase?"

"Three of us, and don't worry, you can trust me, and the rest of them. You'll be safe, I promise you. Skylar can vouch for us, if that makes you feel better," he says, brown eyes pinned on me.

Oddly enough, I believe him. I'm not afraid for my safety around them. I mean they've been my neighbors for over a year and they haven't bothered me once. "Suitcase?"

"We'll get there faster on the bike," he replies with a shrug.

If this means the five-hour drive could be cut shorter, that means I'll get to Ariel sooner. I don't need anything in my suitcase.

"Fuck it," I tell him. "I'll buy new clothes there."

His lip twitches, and he nods toward his black motorcycle. "Get on. I'll try my best to get you there on time."

"Thank you, Renny," I say, grabbing my handbag from my car and crossing the strap over my body. I have my purse, ID and credit cards; anything else can be bought.

"Have you ever ridden before?" he asks as he helps me climb on, his large hands on my waist sending shivers up my spine.

"Yeah, I have actually," I tell him, smiling fondly,

remembering the times I'd ride with my cousin before he passed away. "On the back of one, anyway."

"Okay," he murmurs, studying me with a slightly narrowed gaze. I've always had a weakness for men with blue eyes, but suddenly brown is looking extremely appealing. "I'll skip the debrief then. We need to stop at the clubhouse first, but then we will head off. You have the address of where you need to be?"

"Yeah, I do," I reply, reciting the name and address of the hospital to him.

He nods and hands me his spare helmet. "I'll have your car towed to the clubhouse and it should be ready by the time we get back from Vegas."

"That's great. Thank you," I say, feeling grateful it's one less thing to worry about. "I just need to get there."

The thought of Ariel in labor alone makes me feel sick to my stomach. The baby decided to come two weeks early, otherwise I would have been with her this entire time. The father is my sister's ex and wants nothing to do with the baby, which makes my role even more important.

Renny gets on in front of me and fires up the engine. "Let's do it then."

Feeling awkward, I put the helmet on and hold on to the back of his leather vest, very aware of my personal space, knowing that I'm about to be pressed up against this man for the next few hours at least. I'm not exactly sure how I've found myself in this situation, or how this Renny ended up being my knight in shining armor, but I'm glad he was around.

I've heard a lot of things about the MC—like that they engage in criminal activities and are dangerous womanizers. I know they are judged in the community and that no one wants them here, but I want to form my own opinion. Even the real estate agent who sold me my house told me that he wished they would move away, because they are nothing but trouble.

But from what Renny is doing for me, they don't seem too bad.

Or at least I hope they aren't.

Because I just signed up for the next few hours at their mercy.

Ariel, I'm coming.

Don't miss
Renegade by Chantal Fernando,
available now wherever
Carina Press ebooks are sold.
www.CarinaPress.com